The woman cleared her throat and also backed up a step.

"Are you hungry? Would you like something to eat? My family and I will be eating dinner soon, and you're welcome to join us. I was about to pick some strawberries for dessert."

He opened his mouth to turn down her generous offer, but couldn't force out the words "no, thank you." While the berries were tasty, they were no substitution for a real meal. He hadn't eaten for days, nor did he know where his next meal was coming from. He'd never resorted to begging in his life, but he'd never been so hungry, either.

If God had found a way to give him a decent meal, Elliott would not turn Him down.

"Thank you for your generosity and kindness. I would appreciate that more than words can say."

Her shaky smile warmed his heart, and something went to war in his battered stomach. "You're quite welcome."

"My name is Elliott Endicott, and I'm on my way to where hopefully a job awaits me."

She smiled again, this time with more confidence. "My name is Louise Demchuck. My father is the section foreman here in Pineridge."

Elliott bowed his head. "Pleased to met you, Miss Demchuck."

"Please, call me Louise. We are not formal here in Pineridge. But before we go back to the house, I do need to fill my pail. I think there are plenty of berries here for both of us—for me to pick, and for you to eat."

Elliott had been prepared to help the lady pick, but he discreetly glanced at his hands and decided against it. He could only guess that Louise would not want him handling food she would eat. If he hadn't been so hungry, he wouldn't have eaten food touched with his hands.

The young lady didn't speak as she picked, but instead, she began to hum. Elliott nearly dropped the berries from his hand when he recognized it as "Rock of Ages," his favorite hymn. If he wasn't eating, he would have joined her with a harmony, but then his better judgment reminded him that he was only one of countless, desperate men passing through her town. As such, he was not in a position to develop a friendship with this woman. He probably should not have even spoken to her.

But it didn't matter. Before this time tomorrow, he would be gone on the next freight train.

Gail Sattler lives in Vancouver, British Columbia (where you don't have to shovel rain) with her husband, three sons, dog, and countless fish, many of which have names. She writes inspirational romance because she loves happily-ever-afters and believes God has a place in that happy ending. Visit Gail's website at http://www.gailsattler.com

Books by GAIL SATTLER

HP269—Walking the Dog
HP306—Piano Lessons
HP325—Gone Camping
HP358—At Arm's Length
HP385—On the Road Again
HP397—My Name Is Mike
HP406—Almost Twins
HP433—A Few Flowers
HP445—McMillian's Matchmakers

The Train Stops Here

Gail Sattler

Heartsong Presents

Dedicated to my mother, Helen. Writing this book has been an adventure I'll never forget. Thank you, and I love you, Mom.

Take therefore no thought for the morrow: for the morrow shall take thought for the things of itself. Matthew 6:34

A note from the author:
I love to hear from my readers! You may correspond with me by writing:

**GAIL SATTLER
Author Relations
PO Box 719
Uhrichsville, OH 44683**

ISBN 1-58660-475-9

THE TRAIN STOPS HERE

All Scripture quotatins are taken from the King James Version of the Bible.

All of the characters and events in this book are fictitious. Any resemblance to actual persons, living or dead, or to actual events is purely coincidental.

Cover illustration by Chris Cocozza.

PRINTED IN THE U.S.A.

one

Louise Demchuck pulled her sweater tighter and wrapped her arms around her body to protect herself from the chill of the spring wind as she stood beside the set of parallel tracks. She stared down the metal lengths, searching for the familiar sight of her father sitting on the front of the jigger while the section gang seesawed its double handles, propelling them toward the station. The never-ending lines extended into the distance until they disappeared with the miles. Not detecting any motion, and since the storekeeper's children were not playing outside today after their return home from school, she strained her ears for a hint of sound but heard only the rustling leaves, singing birds, and chirps of the crickets.

She gathered her skirt and ran back to the house. "I don't see Papa or the section men, Mama."

Her mother stirred the soup and sighed. "I suppose the jigger was switched onto the siding, and they'll wait until the train passes. How long will this one stop?"

Louise hurried into the dining room to her father's desk. She ran her finger down the paper with her father's notes of the daily train schedule, which lay in the middle of the desktop, then glanced up at the clock on the wall. If the section gang didn't have enough time to return to the station and get the jigger off the track before the freight train came, then they would have to wait until the train departed before they could return home.

"The 6:15 is a freight train today, so it won't be leaving again until 7:00. I wonder if there will be any hobos on this one."

5

Even from her papa's desk at the front of the dining room, Louise heard her mother's spoon land with a clatter against the metal top of the cookstove in the kitchen. As she knew would happen, her mother's footsteps approached. Louise turned to the doorway between the kitchen and the dining room, and as expected, her mother soon appeared.

Her mother stood glowering at her, arms crossed over her apron. "We do not call them hobos. They are people—people whose lives have met with grave misfortune—from all walks of life, some older than your father, and some the same age as you. They are not traveling for pleasure, or they would be on the passenger train, paying their fare. These are desperate men, Louise. I pray that our family will never be faced with whatever terrible things forced those men to abandon their families and head for parts unknown in the faint hope of finding food and lodging."

Louise's throat tightened. It was true. Many people were out of work. Even for those who maintained their jobs, everyone was spending less money on everything, including food.

With Papa being the section foreman for the railroad, their family had been provided with a comfortable home. Their family maintained the most stable and largest income in their small community.

"You are right, Mama. I hadn't meant to be insulting. It's just that everyone calls them hobos. Even Pastor Galbraith. I didn't mean anything hurtful or mean to speak poorly of anyone."

Her mother shook her head. "It's easy to pass them off by speaking of them in such a way, but the city people don't see the suffering in their eyes like we do. Not even Pastor Galbraith."

Louise nodded and turned to look out the window. The train was due in seven minutes, and without doubt there would be homeless men hiding on it. Some would be riding on top of the cars to avoid being seen from the ground, but once the train stopped, the brakeman would leave the caboose to make his rounds and clear the obvious hiding places. Then, when the shipment for the store owner was unloaded and everything checked and in order, the brakeman would return to the caboose, and the train would start moving. All the hobos would scramble back on, and the procedure would be repeated the next time the train stopped.

A single, long whistle sounded in the distance.

Her mother's words interrupted her thoughts. "It's coming. I can hear it."

Low rumbling and the shaking of the ground signified the train's approach to the station, which was next door to their house.

Knowing her father would not come until after the train departed, Louise hurried up the stairs to her bedroom, where she peered into the distance to watch it, as she had done countless times since childhood. From her window on the side of the house, she watched the big black engine puff out its billow of smoke as the train slowly rolled up to the station.

She could also see the school to the left of the train station, and beside it, the church. On the other side was the bunkhouse for the section gang, which was across the tracks from the station.

Louise smiled. If she went into her parents' bedroom, she could look out the back window and see the entire town of Pineridge. Of course she didn't have to. If she closed her eyes, she could picture every single building, burned into her memory. Including their house, the community consisted of only eight buildings. Directly across the main road behind their house was Mr. Sabinski's general store, and to the west, the home of Mr. Johnstone, the bus driver. Next to that was the service station, owned and operated by Mr. Tolson, who often spent more time out on the farmers' fields fixing the tractors where they had broken down than in his own shop in the town.

Besides those and the homes of the teacher and principal, all else around Pineridge was farms. The only reason tiny

Pineridge could support those few businesses was because very few families besides theirs owned an automobile, and even fewer could afford rail tickets into the city on a regular basis, where prices were cheaper. Since her family received free rail passes, her father went to the city every second weekend for fresh vegetables and meat, and the entire family traveled to the city once a month to shop and visit relatives. Louise appreciated that their family could take advantage of such luxuries.

Louise watched the train as it squealed to a stop. This time, she didn't see men on the tops of the boxcars, but as usual, a few ran from between the cars where they had been hiding on the hitches until the train slowed. One man ran out of a boxcar to hide in the trees before the brakeman began his rounds to clear the train. As section foreman, it wasn't her father's job to evict the hobos from the trains, but if he did see them hiding, he was required to remove them as well, even though they had nowhere to go, especially in Pineridge.

She didn't know those men, but her heart ached for every one of them.

Often, they were so hungry, not having eaten for days, that they came to the house begging for food. Some simply took what was offered, but others asked to work in exchange for the food, even though there was no work for them to do. Of all the men who came to the door begging, none were turned away. Sometimes, when their clothes were so tattered and worn that they could no longer give sufficient protection from the cold nights, her mother gave them pieces of her husband's clothing.

In the summer it wasn't so bad, but for now, even though the last of the snow was gone, the spring temperatures continued to drop sharply to barely above freezing some nights. At this point in the season, her mother had given away most of Papa's warm clothing. Besides his parka, her father now only had one sweater left to his name. Both Louise and her mother knew they would be busy knitting all summer, preparing to give away everything they made to those in need when the colder weather began again.

Whether it was herself, her mama, or her papa who gave the men food or clothing, they always stopped and prayed with them. Most of the time the men listened politely out of obligation for receiving something, but every once in awhile, Louise thought their prayers touched someone's heart. For that reason, she knew that for as long as their family had food to eat, they would share with those who were less fortunate.

She wished she could give away Bibles, but there simply was not enough money to do so. Even if there were, these homeless men could not carry any belongings with them, not even items needed every day. They only had the clothes on their backs. Nothing more.

And week after week, month after month, more and more destitute men passed through the small community of Pineridge on their way to their last hope, a job in some big city, wherever these tracks could take them.

Louise stayed in her room until the train was gone, then returned downstairs to find something to do until her father returned, and they could begin eating their dinner.

❧

Elliott Endicott wiped his mouth and curled into a ball as he lay on the cold wooden floor of the boxcar. He had given up trying to make himself comfortable. It had been so long since he'd last eaten that he'd been sick, except there was nothing left in his stomach to expel. There hadn't been for days. Because he had been on the move for so long and the trains stopped often, he also couldn't remember the last time he'd had a proper sleep.

The whistle sounded and the movement of the train changed, indicating they were approaching and stopping at another station. This time, he would wait until the train was almost at a stop before he moved, because he didn't think he could get up twice. He had never been so weak or felt so ill in his life. He also wanted to move as little as possible because of the filth in the empty boxcar.

His eyes burned from lack of sleep as he watched the movement through the crack in the boxcar door. The train slowed, and he could see he had no choice but to get up and ready himself to jump. As he stood to the side, preparing himself for the right moment, his knees wobbled like rubber, making it necessary to grasp the door frame of the boxcar for support.

The train continued to slow, and Elliott glanced up ahead to see where they were. He could see the train station and across the road what appeared to be a school.

As he neared the set of buildings, Elliott squeezed his eyes shut, trying to block out what had become of him, of his life, and of his dreams.

The second the train stopped, he jumped. He stumbled as he landed, skinning his knuckles, and ran into the trees. If he didn't find berries, he hoped at least to find water to quench a thirst so harsh his throat hurt when he breathed.

Instead of staying close to the station, Elliott wandered down the track and into the bushes, staying out of sight, hoping that if he ventured farther from the main area, he would indeed find berries untouched.

He had sold his watch long ago and therefore didn't know the time. From the position of the sun, he guessed it to be shortly after six in the evening.

Dinnertime. His stomach grumbled painfully at the thought.

Not for the first time, he wondered what would happen once he arrived at his friend Edward's home in British Columbia at the end of his journey, provided he lived to make it. Good or bad, no matter what awaited him would surely be better than this.

Hopefully, he could find something to eat before this train left again. He'd learned the hard way that generally the freight trains traveled in the same direction approximately ten hours apart. The next one to go by would be in the middle of the night. Since this was such a small community, the train wouldn't stop. Elliott calculated that the next train to stop wouldn't be along before noon tomorrow. That being the case, the night promised to be a very cold one with no shelter if he missed getting back on this train. For this moment, he didn't care. He had to find something to eat.

As he wandered farther along the tracks, he recognized the wild strawberry bushes. The bare bushes told him he had not been the first person to discover this patch. However, because of the size of the patch, his heart quickened in the hope that there could be more nearby that had not been consumed by other men riding the freight trains. Elliott made his way farther into the trees, not caring if he came face-to-face with a bear. The bear would have to fight him because whatever he found, he planned to eat.

He hadn't gone too far into the trees before he met with success. Behind an outcropping of rock, he discovered a mother lode of strawberries. Many were green, but others were tender and juicy and begging to be eaten. In the distance, he heard the train beginning to pull away from the station, but he didn't care how cold he would be tonight. He had food.

Elliott sank to his knees in a short prayer of thanks to God for the bounty before him, then grabbed for the berries. At the first bite, he closed his eyes to savor the flavor. They were only wild berries, but he'd never tasted anything so wonderful in his life. They were sweet and tangy and delicious.

He shoveled the strawberries into his mouth as fast as he picked them. One after another, he ate as many as he could, as quickly as he could, not caring that the dark red juice dribbled into his beard. He had over a thousand miles and many days to go before he reached his destination, and he knew he would be much worse for wear by then. Berry stains in his beard would be the least of his worries.

As he reached for more, Elliott's hand froze. From the same

direction he'd come, he heard someone else approaching.

For a second, he didn't want to share his prize, but then he chided himself for being greedy. God had provided, and if God desired, God would take away.

"Papa? Is that you?"

It was a female voice.

The foliage parted. "Papa?" A young woman of about nineteen appeared. She wore a dark green dress that would nearly have blended her into the background if it weren't for her blond hair, as bright as the sun in the dark surroundings. In her hand she carried a dull metal pail.

The second the young woman saw him, her green eyes widened and she backed up a step. She gasped and covered her mouth with one hand, still holding the pail in front of her with the other.

Elliott sprang to his feet. "Excuse me, Miss. Please, don't be frightened. I'm only here to eat these berries and nothing more."

"You were on the last freight train! And it's gone!"

He cringed. He knew it was obvious how he'd arrived, but he was still ashamed. He hadn't seen himself in a mirror recently, but he could guess at his appearance. Neither did he want to think what he smelled like.

Today, for the first time, he had taken the risk of sleeping in a boxcar because the train was in motion. Until only a few hours ago, he had heeded the other men's warnings about the dangers of going into the boxcars. For days he had traveled by scrambling over countless greasy hitches between the cars. He'd ridden many miles from atop the boxcars, which were always heavily laden with dirt and dust, not to mention the gifts from countless birds.

He didn't want to think about the other unmentionables he'd had to deal with inside the boxcar. Without a doubt, in all his twenty-five years on God's earth, he had never been so disgustingly filthy, not even as a child. At least when he was a child, it had been good, clean dirt. However, he'd been so desperate for sleep and protection from the weather that he had taken his chances and actually gone inside when he'd discovered a boxcar with an unlocked door.

He'd never had a beard in his life, and he hated the feel of it. The rough whiskers had grown long enough to be in the bristly stage. Even if it had been long enough to be a cultured beard, he still would have hated it. And, as long as it'd been since he'd bathed or shaved, it was equally as long since he'd combed his hair. No doubt it was matted with things he'd rather not think about.

In addition to everything else, his right shirtsleeve had ripped, and he had no new shirt to change into. His trousers and shoes were grimy, but so far, intact. His shirt pocket had also been ripped when another man had tried to rob him as he slept, leaving a gaping hole.

Unfortunately for both of them, he had nothing the man could steal.

Elliott backed up a step. The last time he'd combed his hair had also been the last time he'd brushed his teeth. "I think I'll find another patch of berries elsewhere."

The woman cleared her throat and also backed up a step. "Are you hungry? Would you like something to eat? My family and I will be eating dinner soon, and you're welcome to join us. I was about to pick some strawberries for dessert."

He opened his mouth to turn down her generous offer but couldn't force out the words "no, thank you." While the berries were tasty, they were no substitution for a real meal.

If God had found a way to give him a decent meal, Elliott would not turn Him down.

"Thank you for your generosity and kindness. I would appreciate that more than words can say."

Her shaky smile warmed his heart, and something went to war in his battered stomach. "You're quite welcome."

"My name is Elliott Endicott, and I'm on my way to where hopefully a job awaits me."

She smiled again, this time with more confidence. "My name is Louise Demchuck. My father is the section foreman here in Pineridge."

Elliott bowed his head. "I'm pleased to met you, Miss Demchuck."

"Please, call me Louise. We are not formal here in Pineridge. But before we go back to the house, I do need to fill my pail. I think there are plenty of berries here for both of us—for me to pick, and for you to eat."

Elliott had been prepared to help the lady pick, but he discreetly glanced at his hands and decided against it. He could only guess that Louise would not want him handling food she would eat. If he hadn't been so hungry, he wouldn't have eaten food touched with his hands.

The young lady didn't speak as she picked, but instead, she began to hum. Elliott nearly dropped the berries from his hand when he recognized it as "Rock of Ages," his favorite hymn. If he wasn't eating, he would have joined her with a harmony. Then his better judgment reminded him that he was only one of countless, desperate men passing through her town. As such, he was not in a position to develop a friendship with this woman. He probably should not have even spoken to her.

But it didn't matter. Before this time tomorrow, he would be gone on the next freight train.

two

"I think I have enough strawberries in my pail now. It's time to go back to the house. Papa should be arriving back very soon, and then it will be time for dinner."

Elliott didn't know which held less dirt, his face or his clothing, but he couldn't stop himself from wiping the berry juice from his mouth onto his sleeve when Louise turned her head. The strawberries had filled a void, but he anticipated dinner like no other time in his life.

"Thank you," he said as he rose and followed Louise through the bushes until they emerged from the trees. She slowed her step for him to catch up, but he hesitated, not wanting to walk beside her in his present condition. However, neither did he mean to insult her, especially considering her generosity. Elliott quickened his pace and walked beside her at what he hoped was a respectable distance, downwind, toward the house beside the train station.

"I won't tell Mama you've eaten your dessert first." She turned to smile at him, and Elliott forced himself to smile back. He'd never felt less like smiling. While he knew she was probably only trying to lighten the moment, it didn't make him feel any better. He'd always said he would rather die than accept charity from a stranger. Now his lofty ideals had been reduced to exactly that—accepting charity versus the harsh reality of dying of starvation. And he'd never considered the possibility of accidental death from the often dangerous predicaments he'd been forced into while riding the freight trains. He would never again speak such words lightly.

Instead of going in the front door, he followed Louise around to the back of the house.

"Please wait here, so I can tell my mother we have a guest."

Elliott's heart sank. A guest. He wasn't a guest. He had been reduced to begging. He was a vagrant. A bum. Or, as the new term dubbed him and other men in his situation, a hobo.

Living as he had been recently gave him an entirely new perspective on what was needed as the bare minimum to survive. He'd been given many lessons in pride and humility like he'd never experienced. Never in his life would he have thought he would be surviving only through the help and sacrifice of anonymous strangers.

While he waited, he tried to figure out where he was. Louise had said they were in a town named Pineridge, but he'd never heard of the place. However, as he'd passed through the countryside, he had also learned a lesson in geography such as he'd never been taught in school.

He'd traveled through countless cities, towns, and communities of varying sizes, but this one had to be the smallest he could remember. From where he stood at the rear of the Demchucks' house, he could only see a handful of buildings—eight total. He surmised that this small outcropping was the hub for the local community of farms in the area.

He found himself staring at the school. Quickly, he turned his head. He didn't want to think about schools. It was only a reminder of what he couldn't have.

Louise stepped outside once again. "Please come in. Mama is heating some water. You can wash up before Papa comes back." She stepped back inside, indicating that he should follow.

In his present condition, he didn't want to go inside their house, but he wouldn't insult her generosity and turn down her invitation. Still, he would much rather have eaten outside than carry his dirt into their home. Elliott inhaled deeply and followed her through the doorway.

As soon as he stepped into the kitchen, the delicious aroma of a fragrant stew caused his stomach to make an embarrassing sound. He automatically covered his stomach with one hand and tried to think about anything other than food.

To distract himself, he glanced around the room. The Demchucks' home was modest but pristine and well cared for. The linoleum floor shone brightly with the sunlight peeking in through the lace-curtained windows. Beside him to his right, just inside the door, stood a small wooden table with a white enamel basin and a bar of soap in a matching dish on top. A colorful floral printed curtain hung from the tabletop to the floor, hiding what was likely a pail beneath. Above the table, a framed mirror hung on the wall.

To his left a woman in her fifties, an older version of Louise, stood beside a large cast-iron cookstove. She wore a dress very similar to Louise's, but the front was covered with a cotton embroidered apron. She turned and smiled at him. "Greetings. Welcome to our humble home."

He forced himself to smile back. "Thank you for having me."

Louise smiled at both of them. "Elliott, this is my mama, Anna Demchuck."

He closed his eyes briefly as he bowed his head in greeting, grateful for the distance between them, because he didn't want her to see how disgusting he was. "Ma'am. Thank you for your invitation. If there is anything I can do for you to return your kindness, please ask."

"Nonsense. God has provided for us well, and all we are doing is sharing it with others in times of need. One day you can return the favor to someone else. I think the water has finished heating. The basin is there beside the door if you'd like to wash up."

There was no if about it. He'd never welcomed soap and water so much in his life.

Without waiting for his response, Mrs. Demchuck brought the basin to the cookstove, ladled some warm water into the basin, and returned it to the washstand.

Elliott stepped back to let her pass. While Mrs. Demchuck settled the basin, he noticed what appeared to be a pump on the floor next to the washbasin table. He tried to be discreet in peeking outside through the window.

An outhouse sat in the corner of the property, confirming the full scope of the Demchucks' lifestyle in a community far away from any metropolitan area. In addition to not having running water, they didn't have indoor plumbing.

In Katona Falls, most homes, although not all, had running water and flushing toilets. He knew that most farms still did not have this convenience, but he had never thought about the smaller communities that weren't quite farms but weren't really a city, either. Now he knew.

Unable to stop himself, he glanced quickly around the room to see what they did have. Next to a large wooden table set with three chairs and covered with a brightly colored oil-cloth, he could see a large stand-up lamp, which confirmed that the Demchuck home had electricity. He also noted a china cabinet, the washbasin and stand, and the large cook-stove, but no refrigerator or icebox.

Still, compared to what he'd seen and done over the past week, their quaint home felt like a palace.

Louise's voice beside him brought his attention back to where it should have been in the first place. "I brought this for you."

Elliott blinked and shook his head slightly. Lack of food and lack of sleep had distracted him from good manners, which was inexcusable. He hadn't noticed Louise leave the room, but now she stood beside him, smiling, holding a clean towel toward him.

"Thank you," he mumbled. Part of him could hardly wait to wash for the first time in longer than he cared to think about, but part of him dreaded it. Now he had to face the mirror and see what he had become.

Mrs. Demchuck removed her apron and slung it across the

back of one of the chairs. "Come with me, Louise; there is something I need your help with in the living room."

In the blink of an eye, the two ladies left the room, and a curtain slipped closed in the doorway leading to the rest of the house. With their departure, everything became so quiet all Elliott could hear was the crackling of the wood in the cookstove.

He suspected they really had no reason to leave the room except to give him some privacy while he did his best to wash. What he really needed was a bath, but he was in no position to do that, especially in the middle of their kitchen at dinnertime. Most important, Louise's father would be returning shortly to find a stranger in his house. Elliott did not want to step any more beyond the bounds of propriety than he already had. Therefore, he decided to hurry to do the best he could to clean himself with the hand soap and small basin of water provided.

Slowly, Elliott turned to the mirror. The man who looked back at him was a stranger. His hair was no longer than it had been a week ago, but in addition to the natural oils of a week of not washing it, it was so dirty it was the wrong color—not his usual neutral brown, but instead, dark and clumpy. He didn't think he'd lost more than a pound or two after eating nothing other than berries for the better part of the past week, except that he hadn't had any extra to lose to begin with. He could feel the difference in the way his clothes fit, but now he could also see it in his face.

He blinked back at himself and looked into his eyes. The mixture of the brown and green that made the hazel color had faded to a dull brown. No doubt because of the lack of sufficient sleep and horrid conditions under which he'd lived, the sockets of his eyes were hollow, yet puffy underneath. He couldn't tell the exact color of his skin; however, his face appeared pale beneath the layer of grime and soot, when he should have had a tan after spending most of his time outside.

He didn't think it was possible, but he looked even worse than he felt.

He squeezed his eyes shut for a second, then stared at himself again as he ran his fingers over his chin, something he'd done countless times over the last week. He'd felt his whiskers grow from harsh stubble to longer, softer hair. The unkempt length disgusted him.

As a teen he'd been proud to be able to sprout a beard quickly, but conversely, as an adult, it now meant he was the first to appear untidy. And now, he noticed as he turned his head, to his dismay, in addition to the dirt, his beard wasn't the same color as the rest of his hair.

The face of the stranger in the mirror made Elliott wish he had access to a razor, but if the best he had was soap and water, he was more grateful for that than words could say.

He worked up a lather in his hands, then rubbed it not only on his bare skin, but into his beard, and then over his hair to get out what grime he could. The blackness of the water turned his already upset stomach, telling him if that was what came off, then he was still very dirty. Trying not to drip water onto the floor, he opened the back door and dumped the dirty water outside and returned the basin to the cook-stove to ladle out more warm water, just as he had seen Mrs. Demchuck do. He walked slowly across the room with the second basin of wash water and washed his hands and face again, this time with better results.

Voices on the other side of the curtain warned him of Louise and her mother's return, so Elliott quickly dried his face and hands. Not knowing what to do with the towel, he draped it over the back of one of the chairs, then froze. Despite having washed twice, he had left smudges of dirt on their nice towel.

Before they returned, he dumped the water into the pail hidden beneath the table, barely having straightened as the curtain opened.

"I'd guess you must be feeling much better?" Mrs. Demchuck asked, smiling so warmly he immediately relaxed.

"Yes, Ma'am. Thank you."

"My husband must be in the middle of a big job that they can't leave, because they're usually back by now. I think we'll begin eating dinner without him today." She picked up the apron and fastened it behind her, and both ladies turned toward the stove.

Elliott wasn't sure what he was supposed to do. If he were a true guest, he would have sat at the table to chat with the man of the house while the women set the food on the table, but he wasn't a guest.

"Is there something I can do to help?" he asked.

Louise carried a loaf of bread and a large knife to the table while Mrs. Demchuck scooped the stew into a porcelain bowl and brought it with her to the table. "This is all there is. We're ready."

He remained standing and pushed in the ladies' chairs to seat them, then sat himself down.

Mrs. Demchuck folded her hands on the table in front of her. "We always give thanks to the Lord for the food we eat."

"As do I, Ma'am."

Her eyes lit up. "Would you like to pray, then?"

He'd never in his life felt more like praying. "Yes, Ma'am. I would."

Elliott cleared his throat, bowed his head, and closed his eyes. "Dear heavenly Father, I thank You for this day and for this wonderful meal before us. Your timing and Your grace is sufficient, as always. I thank You for the bounty which You have provided, for the kindness and generosity of strangers. Today I ask for a special blessing on the Demchuck family as a special thank-you for their willingness to share with a stranger." Elliott paused to clear his throat, which had become tight with a rush of unaccustomed emotion. "Also I ask a special blessing on all the men who have been forced onto the trains, and all people, everywhere, for all their struggles and hardships in these difficult economic times. I pray that You touch every one of them with Your hand of mercy, that they, too, can be provided for, day by day. I ask this in the name of our Lord and Savior, Jesus Christ. Amen."

Silence reigned over the table for a few seconds. Mrs. Demchuck quickly ran the back of her hand over her eyes. "As you can guess, we see many homeless men on the trains. We try to do everything we can for all who ask."

"I can assure you that in the days I have been traveling, I have never met such gracious people as you, Ma'am. I can hardly wait to meet Mr. Demchuck." Elliott paused to smile, and for the first time in a long time, his smile was genuine. "I must admit, I do feel somewhat nervous. After all, he works for the railroad, and I'm not exactly a paying passenger."

Louise pushed the bowl of stew to him, encouraging him to help himself, while her mother began slicing the bread.

Elliott didn't wait for the bread. He spooned out a large but reasonable portion of stew and immediately began to eat. At the first delicious mouthful, he closed his eyes to savor the rich flavors of the meat and gravy but didn't stop chewing while he did so. Ignoring his manners, he spoke as best he could around the food in his mouth. "This is delicious. Thank you, Ma'am."

Mrs. Demchuck smiled and nodded in response. "You're more than welcome."

"Where are you headed, Elliott?" Louise asked as she pushed the plate of sliced bread toward him, along with a bowl of butter.

He tried to swallow quickly, but before he could, Mrs. Demchuck spoke.

"Louise! Let the poor man eat some before bombarding him with questions."

Elliott swallowed. "It's okay. I'm on my way to British Columbia, where hopefully a job in the logging industry awaits me."

"Then you still have many days' travel ahead of you."

"Yes. It took me five days to get here, but now that I've become accustomed to the schedules, and other men have shown me some of the tricks, the rest of the way should be quicker."

Louise grinned. "I can tell you a lot of tricks to riding on the trains, too."

"Louise!"

Louise's mouth quivered. She bit her bottom lip for a second then lowered her head and whispered to him, "I'll tell you later."

"If you still have many days' travel ahead of you, especially if you are going through the mountains, I can assure you that you will be cold. I assume you have no jacket or coat?"

Elliott tried not to cringe as he spoke. He had begun his journey with a good coat and two suitcases full of clothes and his personal effects. Now, all he had left were the clothes on his back, which were tattered and filthy.

He couldn't help himself. He lowered his head and pushed at a carrot on his plate, unable to meet her eyes as he spoke. "No, Ma'am, I don't."

"Then I can give you a sweater of my husband's to help keep you warm. We often give out clothing to those in need. At the same time, we also try to share the gospel as we share food and clothing with the men off the trains. This time, it does my heart good to see you already know the Lord. For you, I especially want to help."

"I don't know what to say. Thank you, Ma'am."

Fortunately, conversation turned to other topics than his personal necessities. If he weren't moving on soon, he would have liked to get to know them better. Besides their generosity in helping him when he needed it, he simply liked them as people. Now, more than ever, he anticipated meeting Mr. Demchuck.

As they talked about mundane, normal topics, the two

women encouraged him to eat another helping of stew, which he appreciated from the bottom of his heart.

After they finished their meal, Elliott didn't know what to do. In Mr. Demchuck's absence, it would have been proper for him to thank them for their generosity and leave, but he had nowhere to go. Even if the next freight train that passed through actually stopped, that wouldn't be until nearly sunrise. There were only two places he could spend the night and not be seen by the residents of the area. He could sleep in the forest alongside the track, where he would be exposed to the cold. Or he could hunch down in the doorway of the train station.

Neither held much appeal, but he didn't have a choice. The sweater would offer some warmth from the cold night but not enough to be close to comfortable. The spring temperatures still dipped quite low after sundown, and the sun was already starting to set.

Something else he had not previously considered—Mrs. Demchuck's kind donation of the sweater forced him to think of the trip through the mountains, where there would probably still be snow on the ground. He didn't want to think of how cold that portion of his journey would be. First, he would worry about tonight. He would worry about what tomorrow would bring tomorrow.

Since the meal was done, Louise and her mother stood. Due to the continuing absence of Mr. Demchuck, Elliott did the same. "Ma'am, I know I've said this before, but thank you again for your generosity. Before I leave, please, is there anything I can do for you?"

She smiled at him as she slipped the apron back on. "Yes, Elliott, as a matter of a fact, there is."

Elliott smiled back. He wanted so much to do something for these kind people. More than anything, he hoped that whatever she was about to ask would in some way be of benefit to the ministry they provided for other men in his situation.

"Anything, Ma'am. Just name it."

"You can stop calling me 'Ma'am.' "

"Yes, Ma'—uh—Mrs. Demchuck."

They smiled at each other.

"That's better. Now if you'll excuse me, I am going to go heat the rest of the stew. I think I finally hear the jigger coming. Louise, why don't you take Elliott into the living room, and you can listen to the radio until your father has finished eating."

three

Louise tried not to let Elliott see her shock at her mother's request to invite him into the living room. Never before had one of the hobos been invited into their home past the kitchen. Some were too awkward to come inside at all, and some were too dirty. Those who did come inside only stayed as long as it took to eat the food given to them, and they never went beyond the kitchen. The men left quickly and quietly once their physical needs were taken care of, hiding until the next freight train came by, and then they were gone from Pineridge forever.

Secretly, it made Louise happy that Elliott had been invited into their home and not encouraged to leave immediately following dinner. Of the countless men riding the trains for whom her family had provided food and clothing, he was not the first to be a Christian. However, beyond his faith, Elliott seemed different than the others, although she couldn't define why.

The majority of the men she'd met who came off the trains had seemed like honorable people. They weren't lazy, nor did they expect free handouts or figure they were owed something for their misfortune. Even though they had fallen on hard times, most of them were riding the trains because they had some specific destination in mind, usually a large city, in the hope of finding a job.

Elliott, it seemed, did not just hope to find a job. From his comments at the dinner table, it sounded as if a job awaited him—he only had to arrive at his destination. She didn't question why he wasn't traveling as a paying passenger if he had a prospective job.

Louise led him through the doorway from the kitchen into

the larger room, half of which served as a dining room, the other half as the living room. His eyes widened as he quickly glanced over everything, taking in the fine furnishings and her mother's beautiful doilies, lace runners, and embroidery scattered throughout. His attention lingered first on the piano in the corner and then on the framed photograph of her family, taken before Louise's sister had married and left Pineridge.

As her mother had suggested, Louise approached the radio. While Elliott studied the family portrait atop the piano, she discreetly swiped off a little dust from the polished wood just above the dial that she must have missed earlier. "Please, sit down. We might be able to catch the 'Jack Benny Show.' Do you listen to Jack Benny where you come from?"

He turned and briefly studied the couch, then turned back to her. "Yes, I do," he said as he smiled. "But if you don't mind, I think I'll stand."

Louise turned the radio on, then turned to face him. During dinner she had noticed the exhaustion apparent in his face. Of course, she had never ridden the trains any other way than in the comfortable passenger cars, but from what her father had told her about how the hobos had to travel, she doubted Elliott had seen comfort since he left home, wherever that was.

"Please," she said, extending one arm toward the couch. "Don't be nervous. Consider us your Christian family and relax. Papa isn't going to lecture you about how you got here. None of the railroad employees like to see people ride the freight trains in such a way, but they also know there is no way to avoid it, so it's going to happen. You look so tired. Please, sit down. I'm sure Papa would love to talk to you once he's finished eating."

He rammed his hands into his pockets. "I do appreciate your hospitality, but I don't want to sit down because I'm so dirty. I don't want to ruin the fine fabric of your couch or leave a mark that will remind you of my presence long after I'm gone."

Louise's throat clogged, and a strange burning sensation began at the backs of her eyes. She didn't know where he came from, but his words made her wonder what horrible situation had caused a man of such a caliber, who would be concerned about soiling their furniture, to be reduced to such means. His concern made her ashamed that her family was doing so well in these troubled times.

"You're so kind to be concerned," she ground out through the tightness in her throat. "I'll be right back."

Quickly, Louise scurried into the kitchen, where her mother was stirring the stew. "Mama, I need a blanket or something for Elliott to sit on. He doesn't want to soil the couch with his dirty clothes. I don't know what to say. He seems so different from the other men who've come through in the past few years."

Her mother nodded. "I know. He seems like an extraordinary young man of good faith and strong character. Your father seems to have been so discouraged lately. I thought that speaking to Elliott would be good for him." Her mother smiled. "I knew you were wondering why I'd invited him in like this."

Louise nodded. "Maybe a little." Abruptly she slapped her hands over her mouth, then shook her head. "I mean, no! I knew you had a good reason."

"Hush, girl. Take the blue blanket from the dresser in your bedroom and throw it over the couch for him."

Louise ran upstairs for the blanket, and she had just returned downstairs as the thumping of the jigger sounded from outside, signifying the return of her father and the section men.

A loud banging sounded on the front door, causing her to nearly drop the blanket. Very aware of Elliott standing not far away, she ran to the door and opened it. Frank, one of the men from the section gang, stood in the doorway, wringing his hat in his hands. "Miss Demchuck, where's your mama?"

Louise's knees turned to jelly. As she wavered, she grasped the frame of the doorway for support. "Papa. . . Is he—?"

Frank shook his head. "No, he's just hurt, but it's bad."

Louise turned to run into the kitchen, but her mother was already running toward the front door, a dish towel clutched in her hand. "What happened? Where is John?"

"We're going to be bringing him in, Mrs. Demchuck. We think his leg's broke. You're going to have to take him to the hospital."

Frank disappeared outside, and after a few agonizing minutes, Frank returned with Henry, slowly bringing her father to the door. Louise and her mother stood aside as Frank and Henry carried her father to the couch, where they laid him down.

Louise had never in her life seen such pain on a person's face, not even when Richard Sabinski fell off the roof of his daddy's store and broke his arm.

"If you need us, just call. We'll be at the bunkhouse."

Without another word, the two men left.

Louise watched as her mother bent over and reached out one hand in readiness to touch his wound but then jerked her hand back. Instead of touching him, she wrapped both arms around her own waist. "How badly does it hurt? Is it really broken?"

He squeezed his eyes shut, pressed his open palm against his lower right leg, then winced in pain. "Probably. A bundle of new ties fell on me. A split second sooner, I might have been killed. Praise the Lord for strange miracles."

Louise watched the change in her father's expression, recognizing the exact moment he realized that a stranger was amongst them.

"Who are you? What are you doing here?"

"My name is Elliott Endicott, Sir. I'm here passing through on my way to British Columbia. Your family invited me in for dinner. I have been waiting for your return so we could talk, but this isn't the meeting I had anticipated. Is there anything

I can do for you?"

"You wouldn't happen to be a doctor, would you?"

"Unfortunately, I am only a barber. But I can drive you to the hospital, if you'll give me directions. I'm assuming you own an automobile?"

"Yes."

Her mother glanced nervously between the two men. "What about your lead hand, Robert?"

Drawing in a deep breath, her father turned to her mother, wincing with the movement and scowling at the same time. "I caught Robert drinking some moonshine when he was supposed to be working. I don't know how I didn't notice sooner, but I guess it's because we were busy. By the time I noticed, he was quite drunk, so I fired him. We were at the end of the shift, getting everything ready so we could leave a bundle of new ties for the section we have to do Monday morning, when Robert tripped and knocked the stack of ties off the jigger and onto me. I couldn't get out of the way fast enough."

Her father turned back to Elliott. "Robert's not going to be driving me anywhere. Are you a good driver, Mr. Endicott? These are all dirt roads here, and it's going to be getting dark soon. The clay is slippery to drive on if it rains, and the clouds are coming."

Elliott nodded. "I assure you, I am a cautious driver, even though most of my driving has been within the city. It's not dark yet, which is good. I don't know where we are or how far it is to the nearest town with a hospital, but I'll gladly do what I can for you. It appears the good Lord set me here at this time for a reason."

Her father started to smile and opened his mouth to speak, but then his smile turned to a grimace, and he sucked in a deep breath of air.

"Can I help you to the car, Sir?"

As soon as her father nodded, Elliott wrapped one arm around her father's chest. Bracing both of them by pressing his other hand into the top of the couch, he then pulled her father up. While leaning on Elliott and balancing on one leg, her father positioned one arm over Elliott's shoulders. In response, Elliott repositioned his arm tightly around her father's waist, and they started moving.

Louise stood in one spot and watched as her mother ran for the keys, while Elliott and her father very slowly hobbled toward the front door. Despite his slim build, Elliott supported her father firmly as they made their way down the steps.

Louise couldn't imagine either herself or her mother trying to move her papa. She and her mother were the same height of five foot two. Her father was a big man, nearly six feet tall, towering over Elliott by a couple of inches, at least. In addition to being so tall, because he worked hard every day, her papa was muscular and, therefore, heavy. She didn't even know how Elliott managed to support her father, but she had a feeling that the fine meal they'd fed him had helped provide the strength required.

While Elliott very carefully helped her father down the front steps one at a time, Louise mumbled a prayer of thanks for Elliott being with them today.

Her mother ran past her, speaking quickly. "I'm going to go to the hospital with them. Take dinner off the stove before it burns. I don't know when we'll be back."

Louise stood on the top step and watched Elliott and her mother make sure her father was able to support himself on one leg while leaning against the railing. When they were assured he wouldn't fall, Elliott ran to the garage, opened the door, and slowly backed the car out. He turned around and drove as close as he could without driving over her mother's flowers. They helped her father into the car, trying to position him so he would suffer the least amount of pain and discomfort, and drove off.

Louise stared blankly down the road long after the cloud of dust settled. The drive to the hospital in Beauséjour would take close to an hour. She didn't know how long it would take to set her father's leg and do the cast, and then the trip home would take them much longer in the pitch-black of the night, so she had no idea when they would be back.

Absently, she gazed skyward and prayed for a cloudless night and that what little light the moon provided could help keep their journey a safe one.

A bang from beside the bunkhouse made Louise flinch. She stopped studying the sky and watched Robert and the men of the section gang carry out a suitcase, a bedroll, a pillow, and a few personal items and throw them into the trunk of Robert's car.

Louise wrapped her arms around herself to ward off the cooling night air, continuing to watch as Henry and Frank struggled to load Robert's heavy radio into the passenger side of the car.

Swaying as he walked, Robert opened the driver's door. He hopped in and the motor roared to life. Robert drove off so fast that his spinning tires created a cloud of dust so thick she couldn't see the bunkhouse while he disappeared down the road leading to the highway.

She thought of Elliott driving her father's car and of both her parents with him. She'd been on that road countless times, and the road was barely wider than one car. She didn't know if Elliott really was a good driver, despite his assurance. However, she did know that Robert was a poor driver, plus, in addition to being angry, he was drunk.

Her stomach clenched so tightly it hurt. The possibility existed that in his angry state, Robert might not care if he ran his former boss off the road.

She squeezed her eyes shut to say a quick prayer for their safety.

Needing to distract herself from the possibilities of her father's car lying in a ditch somewhere, Louise returned inside the house, removed the pot of stew from the stove, and tidied up the kitchen. When all was done, she returned to the living room. Rather than stand and look out the window, she turned off the radio and sat down at the piano to occupy her mind and soothe her fears. It was too early to worry. If morning came and they hadn't returned, then she would have the right to panic.

Alternating between her favorite hymns, Bach, Mozart, and other classical pieces, Louise played until her eyes were sore from concentrating on the paper in the yellow light. She averted her gaze to rest her eyes, but that only drew her attention to the photograph, on top of the piano, of her family, which only served to remind her of their absence.

Louise closed her books, tucked them into the bench, then crossed into the dining room, stood in front of her father's desk, and looked up at the clock hanging above it.

It was nearly midnight, and Louise had never been alone so late at night or for so long. She tried to calm her fears by telling herself that she'd lived here all her life and Pineridge was a safe community. She knew everyone here well. The three men of the section gang were the only changing faces here. Except for Robert, who would not be returning, Frank had lived in the Pineridge bunkhouse for nearly six months, Henry was the last person in the community who was new.

As she had done earlier that same day, Louise went upstairs to her bedroom window and pressed her fingers to the cold glass. She watched out the window, looking for something, anything, to tell her that she was not the only soul still awake in Pineridge.

The only sources of light were the two streetlamps, one in front of the train station, the other in front of the school. Then, a glow appeared in the distance, along with a low hum. Louise smiled and ran downstairs to the door.

They were home. All was well.

four

"Where's Papa?"

Her mother smiled wearily, pushing her hair back from her forehead. "They decided to keep him overnight. We'll have to go back tomorrow to get him. At least the drive will be easier in the daytime. Your father hates that road, and now I remember why we seldom go anywhere at night."

Elliott pushed his fists into the small of his back. "No, it wasn't a pleasure trip, that's for sure. But Mr. Demchuck is being taken care of properly, so that's what's important."

Louise glanced up at the clock, although she didn't know why. "I guess we can ask Mr. Pollack to drive us to Beauséjour tomorrow when we have to pick Papa up."

"We all talked about it, and Elliott is going to stay with us tonight so he can drive me to the hospital tomorrow and bring your father home."

Of course she was glad that Elliott would be driving the car for them, but her relief went far beyond the simple need of transportation for her father.

Ever since the men started riding the freight trains, she had been told of the dangers. The evening freight trains stopped at their station, but the early morning trains only slowed as they passed through their small burg, some well before daybreak, making it very dangerous to climb aboard as the cars moved. She knew that despite the risk involved the men still did it.

Over the past few years she'd watched men who'd wandered away from the tracks in search of food when they missed the evening train. Most of them hid in the trees until the next train came. Of those who came begging for food, it was usually her mother who gave them something, so she didn't often get to meet them. However, the early morning freight trains didn't stop. Her heart had missed many beats watching men falter or stumble while trying to jump onto the moving boxcars. A number of times she had been positive that when the train rolled away she would see a man sprawled across the tracks, dismembered or crushed by the huge steel wheels after missing his mark. So far, that had not happened in Pineridge, but fatalities did occur when men rode the freight trains.

Plus, there were other less obvious but still very real dangers besides being hurt jumping on and off. She'd heard many instances where men were unintentionally locked in the boxcars which were detached from the trains and left in the train yards. The men inside had died because no one could hear them calling out for help.

While she always had been concerned for the safety of the men, they were still strangers and her worries had never been personal. Now that had changed. In the short amount of time since she'd met Elliott, she'd come to know him a little bit as a person—he was no longer a nameless entity passing in the night. She didn't want to think of the many risks he was taking as he made his way to his final destination.

Because her father was a railroad employee, her family received a free rail pass to be used anytime they wanted to travel. Therefore, she couldn't offer him a ticket, because she had none. However, she'd managed to save a small amount of money from working occasionally at Mr. Sabinski's store. Since Elliott wouldn't be leaving until Saturday evening, this allowed her the time to buy him a ticket, although she had a feeling that for his help in driving her father to the hospital and back, her parents would instead be the ones purchasing it for him.

In addition to wanting to be assured of his safety, the delay would give her more time to talk to him, and she dearly wanted to talk. Or, if the last passenger train left before they arrived back from Beauséjour, then he would have to stay until Sunday afternoon. That meant not only would she have another day with him, but he could attend church with her family.

Louise smiled at him, hoping she wasn't being too forward or that he wouldn't get the wrong impression of her words. "That will be nice. It will be good to have you as our guest so we can thank you for doing this for us."

Elliott nodded. "It's not a problem. I didn't give my friend a specific date as to when I would arrive, although admittedly it has taken me much longer than anticipated. If I've calculated correctly where we are, I'm only halfway to my destination. I'm wondering if I could trouble you for some paper and a stamp to write and tell him I'll be there later than my last letter stated. I don't want to further jeopardize the job he's offered me, but at this point all I can do is to send the letter to my brother and have him forward it. I don't have Edward's address memorized, only the directions on how to get there, and I can't put those on the letter."

Out of the corner of her eye, Louise caught her mother attempting to hide a yawn. "I think we should start getting ready to retire for the night. Elliott, I hope you don't mind sleeping on the couch. We can get you a blanket and a pillow."

He smiled, and Louise thought it was a lovely sight.

"Compared to where I've slept in the last few days, your couch is pure luxury."

Her mother smiled back. "But first, and I'm sure you won't argue with this: You, Mr. Endicott, need a bath."

His lovely smile faded, and even beneath the untidy beard, Louise could see his blush. "Yes, Ma'am, I believe I do."

"And one more thing, Mr. Endicott. And I've asked you this before."

"Yes, Ma'am?"

"Please. Stop calling me 'Ma'am.' "

❧

Elliott followed Louise into the basement. He'd never seen anything like it in his life. Instead of a trapdoor in the kitchen floor leading down to a dugout, the doorway to the basement was wide open and had a set of real stairs going down, just like the stairs going up to the bedrooms. This basement ceiling was low, but the room itself was as large as the house. Instead of a dirt floor, the floor and walls were concrete.

The large room was far from empty. Straight ahead he could see a huge round metal tub, and beside it, a smaller metal tub with a washboard inside. To his right as they walked down the stairs, were shelves filled with preserved fruit, and next to the shelves, piles of boxes. To his left sat a large furnace, and next to it, a large woodpile consisting of both logs and broken-up old railway ties.

"There's the washtub."

He nodded and lifted the tub, which was more awkward than heavy. He slung it upside down over his back, and once he got to the top of the stairs, rolled it sideways through the door. He carried it in the same manner all the way to the kitchen, where he put it down near the cookstove.

Mrs. Demchuck straightened from beside a pump on the floor near the back door, where she had just finished filling a pail. She then carried it to the cookstove and dumped it in a large oval container that covered half the top of the surface.

Bathing in a metal tub in the middle of a stranger's kitchen would in no way compare to the relaxing experience of a nice warm bath at home. However, between the late time and his disgusting condition, he couldn't complain, nor did he have the right to compare. Even though he had been born and raised with the conveniences of the city, he thought he remembered a similar tub as a young child. When he was ten, his family had updated to a stationary tub with running water at the same time as the rest of the neighborhood. He appreciated all the work the Demchuck family was doing for him, sharing their best and seeing to his most obvious need, which was to clean himself up.

During the drive to the hospital, he had been embarrassed to think of what it had been like for them to be enclosed with him in the confined quarters of the car for such a long period of time. When they had arrived at the hospital, he'd tried to wait outside since he was far from sanitary, but Mrs. Demchuck insisted he stay with them, as if they had belonged together.

The odd situation had moved him more than he cared to admit. After the death of his parents five years ago, the only family he had left was his brother and his brother's wife and their children. As close as he felt to his brother, he still felt like an outsider when it came to family affairs. Without words, a bond he couldn't explain had developed with the Demchucks. Even if all he could do for them was to drive their car, he would do anything they asked him, simply because of the way they had opened their hearts and home to him.

"Can I carry that pail for you? You must be tired; it's been a long day for you," he said, trying to stifle a yawn of his own, after watching Mrs. Demchuck's yawn. It had also been a long day for him. It had been over twenty-four hours since he'd last slept, and that sleep had not been long or comfortable. He felt himself start to sway at the thought of lying down for a much-needed sleep on their comfortable couch.

Even though he was thoroughly exhausted, the work of carrying the bucket and filling the tub helped to keep him awake, but at this point, he doubted anything could keep him alert.

Louise changed places with her mother at the pump, and Mrs. Demchuck left the room.

"Tell me about where you come from. Is it a big city?"

Elliott could barely think straight, but he tried to describe what he thought were the most interesting aspects of Katona Falls to someone who would never go there. She laughed when he explained that there really was no waterfall there. Often the residents conjectured about how the name of the town came to be, yet they came up with no answers.

Once the washtub contained a few inches of water in the bottom, Louise walked to the cookstove and ladled the water from the oval container into the pail, then dumped it into the tub.

Mrs. Demchuck returned with an armful of clothing. "Here is a clean towel for you, and I've brought you the smallest of what I could find of John's clothes." She laid the pile of neatly folded clothing on the corner of the table. "The soap is on the table with the basin, and I've also brought you a facecloth. If that water is warm enough, we'll leave you alone now."

Louise dipped one hand into the water. "Yes, I think it's fine. Please call us when you're done."

Before he could say anything more, they quickly left the room, and the curtain between the kitchen and dining room slid closed.

He'd never been in such a situation in his life, but he suspected that they were feeling as awkward as he was to have a strange man bathing in their kitchen. He marveled at their trust in him in the absence of the man of the house. No matter how quickly his exhaustion claimed him, Elliott vowed to say a special prayer for them tonight and perhaps every night for the rest of his life.

He quickly removed his soiled clothing and stepped into the tub. The warm water tempted him to relax, but considering the circumstances, he bathed as quickly as he could. By the time he left the tub, his eyes were nearly closing of their own accord.

He discovered the hard way that Mr. Demchuck's clothing was at least two sizes too big for him, but it was clean and warm. Mrs. Demchuck had no doubt compared his frame to that of her larger husband, because in addition to the clothing, she had also supplied a belt and suspenders.

He toweled his hair dry and joined the ladies in the living room. They both lowered their knitting to their laps at the same time.

"Should I assume that the water gets dumped outside?"

"Yes, a few steps beyond the back door we have a small ditch where we dump all the used water."

"You ladies go to bed; I'll do that. I don't know how I can ever thank you for your hospitality."

"Consider it our pleasure. I've left a pillow and some blankets here for you. Sleep well, Elliott."

He nodded. "And you, Mrs. Demchuck, Louise."

Through weary eyes, he could see the hint of a smile from Mrs. Demchuck when he called her by name, instead of "Ma'am."

When the ladies climbed the stairs, he returned to the kitchen and dumped the water in the ditch as she'd explained. With this task accomplished, he aimed himself for the soft, comfortable couch. Once down, he didn't bother to cover himself properly, and he fell into a deep, exhausted sleep.

❧

Elliott slowly became aware that the world was shaking. A rumble that grew to a loud roar tried to separate him from his dreams, but what finally pulled him out of his sleep was the heavenly aroma of frying bacon and fresh coffee.

With a start, he sat up, discovering himself tangled in blankets, on a couch, in a living room he didn't recognize. As the world came into focus, he realized that the shaking and the roar was from a train going by.

He blinked, and slowly the events of the day before played over in his head like the script of a movie, except that everything was in color.

As quickly as he could, he gathered his thoughts and folded the blankets. He wasn't sure where he was to leave them, and as he looked around the room contemplating the best place, he spotted a man's jacket hanging over the chair next to the desk.

Elliott smiled at Mrs. Demchuck's thoughtfulness. He slipped on the jacket, exited the house, and walked around to the back of the property to the outhouse. Over the past few days he thought he'd become used to the cold, but after only one night in a warm house, the morning air chilled him to the bone. Never again would he take indoor plumbing for granted.

Once he returned inside, he draped Mr. Demchuck's jacket over the chair and entered the kitchen.

"Good morning, ladies."

Mrs. Demchuck turned to him. "And a good morning to you. Did you sleep well, Elliott?"

"Yes, I did. Thank you, Ma'—Mrs. Demchuck."

At his near slipup, Louise made a strange sound, covered her mouth with her hands, and turned away.

Elliott couldn't look away. Yesterday, since he had been so tired, he had poured all his concentration into trying to help them. By the time they'd arrived back at the house, he could have fallen asleep on the hard wooden floor, but instead, he'd had to take a bath. He'd been so tired he had barely been able to keep his eyes focused. He didn't remember making it to the couch, but obviously he had.

Today, he felt like a new man. Most of all, he could think clearly.

The first thing that popped into his mind was that he hadn't properly dealt with Louise. Yesterday everything had happened so fast, and, before he knew it, he was waking up on their couch.

In too short a time, the next freight train would be pulling away from their little burg, and he hadn't yet properly expressed his thanks for all Louise and her family had done for him. If he and Louise had met any other way, he would have liked to get to know her better. But, since he was in the middle of nowhere and would never pass this way again, developing any sort of relationship, even a simple friendship, could only lead to hurt and disappointment. When the time came for them to separate, it would be forever.

Still, if all he had was until dinnertime when the next freight train passed through, he wanted to make the most of it.

"What time is it?" he asked.

"It's nearly ten o'clock. You've apparently slept in."

Mentally, he counted on his fingers. By the time they ate, then drove to the hospital and back, it would be midafternoon. He didn't know if the freight trains kept the same schedule on the weekend. Actually, the more he thought about it, he really wasn't positive that this was the weekend. Something deep inside hoped that today's schedule would allow him more time to stay, even if it meant a colder ride due to a later hour.

"Dare I ask, what day is it?"

Louise's eyebrows quirked up. "Today is Saturday."

Mrs. Demchuck turned from her place at the cookstove. "Breakfast is almost ready. Would you like to have a seat?"

He glanced quickly to the table, which was already set for three. Elliott lowered himself into one of the chairs and waited while Mrs. Demchuck brought the frying pan to the table and portioned the food onto the plates.

"Checkout time at the hospital is noon, although it won't take nearly as long to get there as it did last night."

Elliott looked up to the clock on the wall. "What time should we be leaving, then?"

"Actually, if I have to go this time, I won't have enough time to prepare dinner. Since everything is under control and he's now coming home, I thought that I would stay here, and Louise can go in my place to give you directions to the hospital. I doubt you'd remember your way after that awful trip in the dark." She turned to her daughter. "Louise, do you mind?"

five

Elliott backed the car out of the garage, then got out and ran around to open the passenger side door for Louise. She smiled hesitantly at him as he held the door open for her and slid in, carefully tucking her skirt beneath her before he pushed the door closed.

He quickly ran back around, grinning as he made a point of glancing at the only road in and out of the small burg. "I don't think I need directions to get out of Pineridge," he said as he began the trip down the long, narrow dirt road.

She grinned back. "No, I don't suppose you do. I guess where you come from is much bigger than this. Cat—something Falls, where there are no falls?"

He smiled. "Katona Falls. Because it was dark and we were in such a rush, I didn't see much of the city on the way to the hospital. I think Katona Falls is much bigger than Bows. . .uh. . .I really can't remember what it is, much less pronounce it."

Louise laughed, and it was a delightful sound. She pretended to tie a bow tie at her throat. "Bows. Now think zees." She pointed to her lower lip, letting her mouth open wide as the next syllable came out. "Zuh." Lastly, she pressed her teeth together at the same time as pursing her lips, the last syllable coming out between her teeth. "Zhure. Beauséjour. It's a French name. I don't speak French, nor do I know what it means, but I can pronounce that one word." She grinned widely. "After a little practice, mind you."

They laughed together as she continued to coach him with the correct pronunciation until he got it right. As they continued on, they talked about many things, yet nothing in particular for the length of their journey. Elliott couldn't remember the last time he'd enjoyed himself so much.

He also couldn't believe how soon they reached the town limits, compared to the grueling expedition the previous evening. While the trip would have taken longer at night, he knew the companionship had made the difference. He found himself very disappointed that within minutes they would be at the hospital, and his time alone with Louise would be over.

As soon as he parked the car, he ran around to Louise's door and opened it for her. She turned to enter the small hospital building, but he touched her arm, stopping her midstep.

"This probably isn't the best time to ask, but since this will likely be the last time we will have alone together, I want to ask if I may write to you once I'm settled into my new job? Within a few hours I'll be gone, and I feel there is so much more we have to say to each other."

Her eyes widened, making Elliott think he had never seen such pretty eyes. Her cheeks darkened, and she lowered her head and stared at the ground. "Yes, I think I'd like that. Our address is very simple, just Pineridge, Manitoba. Everyone knows everybody else, and the post office is at Mr. Sabinski's store. We don't need to use the addresses or anything like that."

He escorted Louise to her father's room, where they found him perched on the side of the bed talking to a nurse. Mr. Demchuck smiled as soon as he saw them enter the room.

He held up a pair of crutches. "This is harder than it looks."

The nurse crossed her arms over her chest. "We wanted our patient to stay another day, but he insists on going home."

Mr. Demchuck shook his head. "I have work to do. I don't have a lead hand to take over for me. No one will have done the track inspection this morning, and I can't leave it unchecked another day."

The nurse tapped her foot, her arms still crossed. "I'm sorry, Mr. Demchuck, but I'm afraid that's impossible. You won't be doing any work for awhile. You might be up more in a week when you get used to the crutches, but even then, you'll find movement quite exhausting. And if you fall. . ." The nurse shook her head. "I don't want to see you back here with a broken arm in the next few days. You'll heal best if you rest. Do I have to call for the doctor?"

"I can only rest once the track is taken care of and I'm at home. Louise, did your mother give you the money to pay for everything?"

Louise pulled an envelope out of her purse and handed it to her father. Mr. Demchuck counted the money inside and nodded. "We'll be leaving then."

The nurse scowled, but at the same time, one corner of her mouth crooked up, and she cleared her throat.

Elliott leaned closer to Louise so he could whisper. "Is he always like this?"

She nodded very slightly. "Yes, but it's not what it seems. We've been here before when members of the section gang have been hurt, and most of the nurses know Papa. This is the first time he's been hurt, so it's a little different this time. They know he likes to tease, but they also know when he is being serious."

"He's being serious, now?"

She nodded again. "Yes. With Robert gone, there isn't anyone to oversee the track if Papa isn't there, and it's crucial that the inspections be made daily."

The nurse helped Mr. Demchuck into a wheelchair, and Elliott and Louise walked beside him as they proceeded to the front desk, where Mr. Demchuck paid the bill. The nurse pushed the wheelchair until they were all the way to the car. When Mr. Demchuck was steady on his crutches, she reluctantly allowed him to dismiss her and wheeled the chair back toward the hospital.

Elliott opened the passenger door, then helped Louise's father steady himself beside it before he ran around and climbed inside. Elliott crawled across the seat on his hands and knees, and as best he could from the awkward position, he helped Mr. Demchuck to lift himself inside. At first Mr. Demchuck appeared to be doing fine by himself. He pulled himself into the car backward, keeping one hand on the back of the seat. He braced his other hand on the dashboard, while maneuvering his leg. The heavy cast made the task awkward at best. He had almost pulled himself up enough to slide the rest of the way on the seat when he bumped his bare toes on the metal car door. Mr. Demchuck recoiled from the pain, causing him to lose his grip on the back of the seat. He frantically tried to right himself, but he began to slide down.

Louise dropped her purse on the ground and raised her arms, as if she could do something to prevent him from falling. The vision of Mr. Demchuck falling on Louise and both of them being hurt flashed through Elliott's mind.

Without thinking, Elliott lunged forward and grabbed Mr. Demchuck under the arms, then half pulled and half dragged the poor man all the way onto the seat.

Mr. Demchuck swiped his arm across his forehead. "I still seem to be a little dizzy. Those painkillers must have affected me more than I thought. Thank you, Elliott. That was a close one. I had no idea it was going to be this difficult, but I have to go home today. Waiting won't make it any better tomorrow."

"No, Sir, I don't imagine it will."

Once her father had properly positioned himself, Louise climbed up into the seat and squeezed into the small remaining space. She tucked her legs in so she wasn't touching her father's cast, then pulled the door closed. "I'm ready. We can go home now."

Elliott drove as carefully as he could. The roads in town were fairly smooth, although there were many winter potholes to maneuver around. The highway, being concrete, allowed him to reach a good speed of 30 mph to make the journey in as little time as possible. Very little was said as they traveled along, and the silence started to make Elliott uncomfortable.

He cleared his throat. "This is a fine car, Sir."

Out of the corner of his eye, he saw Mr. Demchuck nod once and smile. Immediately, Elliott relaxed.

"Yes, it's a 1932 Ford Cabriolet with one of those new eight-cylinder block engines. I suppose you have noticed how smoothly it runs."

"Yes, Mr. Demchuck, it does. Shifts easily, too."

"It has a 65-horsepower engine, and I only paid $610 for it, brand-new."

Elliott checked the odometer. "It doesn't have many miles on it for a six-year-old car."

"No, generally the only place I drive is to Beauséjour, and that's not very often. We take the train to Winnipeg twice a month to do our shopping. Other than that, there really isn't anyplace to go. We don't even have to drive to church; it's right in Pineridge. However, it's too small to have our own minister, so one minister travels around to many such community churches around the farming areas. Some services in the area are Saturday, but we've been blessed to actually have our service on Sunday at two in the afternoon. Do you have to travel far to your own church?"

Elliott forced himself to smile. The stock market had crashed when he was only sixteen. He'd been old enough to remember better times, but too young at the time to realize why they could no longer buy the things they had when he was younger. As he grew into adulthood, the economy continued to worsen and unemployment steadily increased. Instead of following his dreams, which included going to university and owning a car of his own, he had to work at his family's barbershop. Because he couldn't afford a car, he'd bought a motorcycle. Then, as times continued to worsen, he'd had to sell the motorcycle, among other things he'd valued, just to have enough money to pay for his food and other needs. Lately, the only time he drove, versus walking, was when he drove his brother's car when they needed supplies for their shop.

He faced straight forward as he spoke, concentrating more on the road than he needed to. "At home, I attend services at a church within walking distance from home."

"Louise plays the piano, so she plays the organ at church. She plays well."

"Thank you, Papa. You know I enjoy it."

They continued in silence until Elliott slowed to turn down the road that led to Pineridge.

"Elliott, while you're here, I was wondering if you could do something else for me. I hate to ask this, but I'm stuck. I need someone to inspect the track."

"Inspect the track, Sir?"

"Yes. It is my duty as section foreman to inspect my thirty-mile section of track every morning. It's also critical that I check and test every switch, every day."

"I'd be glad to, but I'm not sure what to do."

"You'd look for loose or broken spikes and ties that have split or become deteriorated. Then you'll have to mark those for the section gang to replace the next day. Any dead animals or debris must be cleared immediately, because any debris could cause an accident or derail the trains. Switches must be checked to be sure they are operating perfectly, including filling up the indicator lights with coal oil. When I do the inspection on my own on the weekend, it usually takes only a few hours."

Elliott had seen a clock on the wall at the hospital, and he estimated the time to now be about half past noon. He tried to calculate when they would arrive back at the house, then how much longer for him to receive adequate instruction for such a task. If the job took an experienced man a few hours, he didn't know how long it would take him, when he wasn't sure what he would be looking for. He suspected it would be much longer. Still, he couldn't say no, not in light of the present circumstances. "I'll do my best, Sir."

"I know what you're thinking. You're trying to figure out if that will give you enough time to hop back on the next freight train, and it might not. I want you to forget about that. For your trouble, I want you to spend the night with us again. Come to church with us tomorrow, and then I'm going to buy you a ticket on the passenger train for your kindness in helping us. Anna tells me that you have a job waiting for you on the coast. You'll get there faster with a paid ticket, even leaving a day later, than riding the boxcars."

"I don't know what to say, Sir."

"Well, there is one thing you can do."

"Yes, Sir. Anything."

"This is Pineridge, not the city where you came from. You can stop calling me 'Sir.' And don't call me Mr. Demchuck, either. My name is John."

Elliott bit his lower lip. Out of the corner of his eye, he saw Louise trying to hold back a giggle. Today, he was alert enough not to make the same mistake as he'd made with her mother. "Okay. . ." He nodded once, slightly. "John."

Upon their arrival at the house, Elliott drove the car as close as he could to the door and did his best to help John climb out. Elliott knew that even long after he left their home, he would always struggle to think of the man by his first name, as he hadn't been raised to address men old enough to be his father in such a manner.

Rather than have either of the women help John up the stairs, Elliott hurried to park the car in front of the garage, then jogged back to help John balance with the crutches up the three steps and get into the house. Once inside, he followed John to the couch and helped lower him as gently as he could until John was seated as comfortably as possible. Even still, John was short of breath for a few minutes.

"I'm not going to be able to do much, but I figure if we can do the inspection today and all is perfect, it should go smoothly tomorrow. We never miss a day of inspection unless it's an emergency, but both Frank and Henry are gone for the weekend, and Robert is gone for good. Monday they'll be back, so I can make arrangements for them to help until I'm out of the cast. For this weekend, I don't have a choice but to ask you to help. Usually, when I'm with the section men, we use the jigger, but since I can't put the speedster on the tracks, you're going to have to."

Elliott had no idea what a speedster was, but in the back of his mind, he could vaguely picture what a jigger looked like. He'd occasionally seen them, but he'd never been up close to one. He knew jiggers had wheels large enough to fit on the train track, and that in structure a jigger was basically a platform on wheels with some kind of double-handled pump in the middle, which was used to propel the unit. He didn't know what a speedster was, but if it was anything similar to a jigger, he had to assume it also would be constructed of mostly metal, and therefore, it would probably be heavy.

"Put it on the track? Has it fallen off?"

"No, no." John shook his head. "During the day, when we're working, we have it on the siding, but we can't store it on a siding when it's not in use."

"Siding?"

"That's about a half-mile section of track which runs parallel to the main track. It's operated by a switch, and one train uses it to park to allow another train to pass by. We also use the siding to park our jigger while we work. I do the same with the speedster when I'm alone."

"Oh. Then where is this speedster now if it's not on a siding?"

"It's in the toolhouse around the back of the bunkhouse. The railroad doesn't put in a length of track just to move the jigger, and especially not the speedster, so we pull it off the track at night and push it into the toolhouse."

Elliott tried to picture the procedure and couldn't. "Can this be done by one man?"

"There are ties laid out so it can be pushed on a solid surface, like a bridge, if you will. That way it won't sink into the ground. From the shed to the track is about fifteen feet. At the end, we've got the ties parallel to the track, so we only have to lift it sideways and put it on the track from beside. I do it myself every weekend."

For now, Elliott sat eye-to-eye with John, but since he was wearing John's clothes, he knew exactly how much bigger John was than himself. John had to outsize him by three inches in height and a good thirty pounds in weight. Of more importance than the difference in physical size, by trade Elliott was a barber. He knew he was too thin, but more so, he didn't do much in the way of physical labor. He didn't want to embarrass himself by being unable to do the task.

He cleared his throat. "I'll do my best, but I will need instructions."

"I can go with you. I figure if I can get into the car, I can get onto the speedster, which is lower than the seat of the car. We'd have more room on the jigger because the speedster is only meant for one, but one man can't move the jigger. And if we're going to do it, we should do it now. We have to keep the schedule in mind, and we can't afford mistakes. They could be deadly with a train coming on the same section of track."

Elliott stood. This wasn't something he was looking forward to doing, but putting it off wasn't going to make the situation go away.

John lifted one arm to brace himself on the back of the couch, stiffened, but didn't push himself up. "Louise, did you by any chance get the schedule today?"

"Yes, Papa, I did." She turned and walked to the desk, picked up a piece of paper, and returned with it, handing it to John, who relaxed and skimmed it.

He rested the paper in his lap, then lifted his head to face Elliott. "Every morning at seven o'clock they give everyone down the line the daily schedule by phone."

Elliott turned his head slightly toward the desk and felt his cheeks heat up. It wasn't realistic to expect any degree of privacy in the middle of the living room of such a small house, but it embarrassed him to know that Louise had been in the room with him, on the phone for quite some time only fifteen feet away. Even if she hadn't meant to, she couldn't have helped but watch him as he slept. He'd been so exhausted he wondered if he slept with his mouth open or, worse, if he snored. "I didn't realize I was that tired. I didn't hear the phone ring."

Louise shook her head and smiled. "It doesn't ring. The phone is only hooked up between the dispatch office in Kenora and the other section houses along the rail line. We have to be at the desk to listen at precisely seven o'clock every morning. It's difficult to hear clearly at times, but we have to be accurate in case there is a change in the schedule. Papa has to be sure the section gang and the jigger are off the main line and that they don't have a tie pulled out without a replacement at the time the trains are scheduled to pass by. He also needs to know if the trains are stopping, as time has to be allowed for the mail to be transferred and passengers to get off or board. After all, with only one store, the freight trains don't stop here that often. Nor do we often have passengers stopping."

Elliott couldn't imagine a community so small that the trains wouldn't necessarily stop, but it was so in Pineridge. The town, if he could call it a town, was no different in the daylight than it was in the dark. He'd counted exactly eight buildings here, and that included the train station.

John lowered his head to read the paper. "There's going to be a passenger train going through in about ten minutes, then the next train won't be by for three and a half hours, which is a good time to do the track inspection. We should go now and start getting ready to move the speedster." Once more, John braced himself against the back of the couch, but this time, he actually rose. Elliott stood in front of him, prepared to help if required.

When John was standing and leaning properly on the crutches, he turned and called out to the kitchen. "We'll be back in plenty of time for dinner, Anna. If you wouldn't mind, can we take those sandwiches you made for lunch with us? I believe Elliott and I have a lot of work to do."

six

Not caring that her mother could see what she was doing, Louise stood at the kitchen window to watch Elliott and her father as they slowly made their way to the toolhouse. Her heart clenched to see how carefully Elliott helped her father position the crutches in order to make his way across the tracks. She could only imagine how difficult it would be to maneuver over the rails and not have the crutches slip while going over the ties, to say nothing of going over the loose rocks that surrounded the tracks. Watching how Elliott diligently did everything he could to help her papa nearly brought tears to her eyes. She didn't want to think that by this time tomorrow, he would be gone. Her only consolation was that he had promised to write. For anyone else, she would have questioned the sincerity of such intentions after such a short time spent together, but for Elliott, she knew he would keep his word.

Her mother's voice behind her made Louise jump. "I'll miss him, too. He seems like a fine young man."

Louise felt her cheeks burn with the realization that her mother knew what she was thinking. "Yes. I hope I will be able to sit beside him in church tomorrow."

"I don't see why not. Your father appears to like him."

The long whistle sounded, announcing the approach of the passenger train, right on time. Her mother joined her at the window, and together they watched the Transcontinental, which never stopped in a place as small as Pineridge, go by, momentarily blocking their view of Elliott and her father.

After the train passed, they watched as the men continued to make their way past the bunkhouse and to the toolhouse.

"He says he's a barber, Mama. I could tell he didn't know

what Papa was talking about."

Her mother nodded. "I know. And he's so thin. I don't know how your papa expects that Elliott will be able to move the speedster by himself."

They watched at the window in silence as Elliott pushed the speedster down the row of ties, then struggled to lift it onto the tracks.

"I think he's going to need some liniment tonight."

Louise nodded. "Yes."

She remembered back to the previous night when he had offered to do some work, any work, in order to pay them back for providing a meal for him. She doubted he had any idea of the kind of work they did here to maintain the track. In a way, she wondered if Elliott was sorry he'd asked, but the more she thought about it, she doubted that he had any regrets, no matter how sore she knew he would be in the morning.

"Look, Louise! He's done it!"

She also caught him pressing his fists into the small of his back when her papa wasn't looking.

Next, they watched as Elliott braced himself, allowing her papa to use him for stability to push himself up onto the speedster. Struggling with the crutches, her father half pushed and half lifted himself onto the small seat; and Elliott hopped onto the back of the speedster's platform, barely managing to stay on, as the small unit was only made for one person. Her father pointed to a few things on the control. Elliott nodded, then pushed down hard on the handle to get the speedster moving.

Very slowly, the speedster began to inch forward, then pick up its pace. Louise and her mama watched as it disappeared down the length of track.

"I think we've done enough dillydallying, Louise. It's time to start cooking dinner. Can you fetch some meat from the outdoor cellar? I think today we'll have a nice roast beef and mashed potatoes."

Louise slipped on her boots, then her sweater, and went

outside to unlock the trapdoor beside the garage. She fastened the buttons to her neck, then descended the steps into the outdoor cellar. She saw that since more of the snow which she had packed down in the winter had melted with the warmer weather, she needed to lower the strings on the pails containing the meat, as a few were now more than a few inches from the snow-packed floor.

From one of the hanging pails, she selected a nice-sized roast beef that her father had purchased on his last trip to Winnipeg and quickly ran back up the stairs, outside, and back into the house where it was warm.

As she deposited the roast on the table, her mother laid an armload of clothes on one of the kitchen chairs.

"While they're gone we can get the ironing done. Since I had to wash Elliott's clothes while you were gone to Beauséjour, I also washed some of your papa's things. You can start ironing, and I'll go fix the holes in Elliott's shirt, now that it's dry. Plus, I also have some other mending to do."

Louise rested the iron on the cookstove to heat it, then brought the ironing board up from the basement to begin her chore. While she ironed, she listened to her mother work the treadle of the sewing machine, which was in the dining room under the window.

She could tell the difference between ironing her father's trousers and those belonging to Elliott. Still, she realized that even with the difference in size, Elliott's smaller-sized clothing didn't fit as they were meant to. She wished there were some way to send food with him. She also hoped that when he left he would take full advantage of the fine food on the dining car during his long trip to the coast. It made her heart ache to think that it wasn't simply because he was single that he didn't cook properly for himself. The reason he was so thin was because he couldn't afford enough food.

"Mama," she called out, "are you going to cook lots of extra potatoes since we have a guest?"

Her mama appeared in the doorway, Elliott's shirt in her hand. "Yes, Louise. It breaks my heart to see him so thin. I only wish he was staying longer."

"As do I, Mama, but to wish that way wouldn't be fair. He does have a job to get to, and he's been so kind to stay and help us."

The daily track inspection didn't take much longer than usual, and the men returned with plenty of time before dinner. However, instead of sitting in the living room as Louise expected, they both went to her father's desk.

Elliott pulled one of the dining room chairs to the desk, positioning it so her father could have his casted leg extended. Her papa's left leg was tucked partway under the desk, giving him access to the desktop if he leaned sideways in the chair. Louise didn't want to think that he was as uncomfortable as he looked. The doctor had told them he would be in the cast for eight weeks, and they would be long and miserable weeks. Of that, she had no doubt—not only for her father, but likely for the rest of the family as well.

Elliott sat at the regular desk chair off to the left side, also straddling the desk on his own side. With his right leg under the desk and his left leg sticking out, he didn't look comfortable either, but the strange position allowed both men access to the small desktop at the same time. As her father talked, Elliott made notes. They frequently stopped to read from the paper, talk about it, then continue on with her father talking and Elliott writing once again. At times, they stopped talking and writing entirely and examined other leaflets and books her father used for the railroad's records and schedules.

Louise finished the ironing and then began preparing a cake, which would go into the oven as soon as the roast was removed, so they could have something sweet for dessert. They had decided Louise would make her favorite—a special honey cake, made from honey purchased from one of the farms in the area.

Instead of staying in one spot to iron, she now could only sneak peeks at Elliott and her father as she walked back and forth while she did her baking.

Elliott and her father continued to mull over the papers at the desk. She strained her ears to hear what they were saying, but she could hear only the muffled murmur of low male voices, since they were facing the wall as they worked. Occasionally, she could make out the odd familiar word while they discussed the daily track inspection, but yet, the conversation seemed to be more detailed than she ever remembered when she overheard her father discussing the same things with the men from the section gang or even Robert, his former lead hand.

"Louise, I think we're going to eat in the dining room today, since we have a guest and this is the only time we'll have the opportunity to seat the four of us together for dinner."

Louise smiled. She could barely believe that only one day ago Elliott came into their lives as a hobo off the freight train. In that short space of time, she'd come to know him as a man of character and fine upbringing, regardless of the method of his arrival or his current situation. Also in that short space of time, he'd earned a special place in her heart, something he would never know.

Just as she entered the dining room to begin setting the table, Elliott and her father rose. Instead of going into the living room, Elliott followed her father outside. He stood on the steps and allowed her father to support himself by leaning on him as they hobbled down the steps together. Side by side, the two men made their way to the outhouse.

Her heart ached to see her father require assistance with such a simple thing as going outside and wished it didn't have to be so. She knew what it was like to have indoor plumbing from when they visited friends and relatives in the cities. Now knowing more about where Elliott had come from, it embarrassed her to think of how primitive their lifestyle appeared to him.

More than the simple necessities, seeing her father's difficulty with the few steps in the front of the house brought to the forefront of her mind how difficult it would be for him to climb the stairs in the house to go to his bedroom.

The more she thought about it, the more worried she became that neither she nor her mama would be able to do everything necessary for him, even the simple tasks of helping her father move around their own home.

As Louise set the dining room table, she tried to close her mind to the problems of the future. She stopped all her motions and quoted Matthew 6:34 in her head, only letting her lips move, with no sound coming out as she prayed. "Take therefore no thought for the morrow: for the morrow shall take thought for the things of itself."

Before she opened her eyes, she heard the clunking and banging of the men coming back up the stairs, reminding her to add a thanks to God for the blessings they had received in having Elliott with them for the past day and especially for his willingness to help. Elliott may have thought they were helping him, but so far, he had helped them more than he could ever know. She only hoped Elliott knew how much his help and presence had come to mean to them.

As soon as the door opened, her mother walked through the doorway from the kitchen, wiping her hands on her apron as she spoke. "Please go straight to the table. Everything is ready now."

Louise helped her mother bring the food to the table, her father prayed over their food, and they began to eat. During the mealtime, Elliott and her father bantered back and forth good-naturedly about the track inspection, and Elliott playfully groaned out loud when her father reminded him that they would have to do the same thing the following morning, only this time, they would do it early in the morning, at the time it was supposed to be done.

Elliott first laughed at her father's joke about being awake and ready at seven o'clock to listen to the daily schedule on Sunday morning, but then suddenly, his laughter and his smile faded.

"Wait. Are you saying that you also must do this on Sunday?"

Her father also lost his smile, and suddenly the house became very quiet except for the distant crackle of the wood in the cookstove.

"It's necessary to inspect the track every day, including Sundays. The trains never stop running. Either a passenger train or a freight train comes through every few hours, every day, even Sunday. Therefore this is for the safety of hundreds of people who will be on the trains on Sunday. I liken it to a farmer, who must do certain tasks every day in order to keep the farm running and the animals healthy. Only that which cannot be left is done, and the rest of the day is set aside for the Lord's Day."

"I see."

A silence remained over the table, until Elliott cleared his throat and continued.

"Unfortunately, in our modern society, there are many things that must carry on, even on Sundays. Times are changing, and after being with you for only the one inspection, I understand what you mean about things that cannot be left. You said that your worship service in Pineridge is in the afternoon. That does allow you to put aside the majority of the day for our Lord to the best of your ability. I'm sure God honors that."

Her father nodded. "This job is one of few that gives us daily opportunities as a family to be able to help others who are less fortunate. We see homeless people every day. Even though it's only one stop and one day in their journeys, I like to think that the good we do for them can make a difference. Without this job, the home, the good wage, even down to the wood the railroad provides for us, we couldn't do that."

Elliott's cheeks darkened below his beard. "Yes. I'm a testimony to that."

Louise remained silent, but her mother spoke up. "We'll never know if the one thing we do for those who ask will help lead a lost soul to salvation, but we trust that this is what the Lord would have us do."

Briefly he turned his head, making direct eye contact with Louise. She froze, her fork lifted halfway to her mouth, and stared back. His gaze remained fixed as he spoke. "Only the Lord knows what my stop here has meant to me." He paused for a few seconds, then turned back to her mother. "You truly do have a wonderful ministry here, both for the Christian and the nonbeliever."

Louise thought her heart might pound out of her chest. She wanted to say that she also knew that this time was special in a way she still couldn't figure out, but she didn't want to say anything in the presence of her parents and especially not at the dinner table.

Fortunately, the conversation continued with Elliott sharing some of his experiences while riding the freight trains. His tales were fascinating, but at the same time they drove pangs of sadness into her heart to hear of such heartbreaking testimonies. Elliott mentioned many men he'd met. Though times were difficult, they all shared an underlying thread of hope—hope that when every man arrived at his destination, wherever it might be, he would also find a job and the means to a better life.

As soon as everyone was done, before anyone left the table, Louise rose, scurried into the kitchen, and returned with the cake she'd made.

Elliott stared at it as if he'd never seen a cake in his life.

Louise smiled from ear to ear. "This is my favorite cake. I hope you like it. It's a honey cake."

"I don't know what to say. I can't remember the last time I had a piece of cake. Saying thank you doesn't seem like enough for the way you've opened up your home and welcomed me like a friend."

Regardless of the fact that her parents were there, or perhaps because of it, she allowed her fingertips to rest lightly on his arm. "We're welcoming you as a Christian brother, as well as a friend."

He looked up at her, and all thoughts of cutting the cake fled Louise's mind. Not even when they helped her father at the hospital and not even when they were alone together in the car had she been so close to him. This was the first time she truly looked closely at him, and she was mesmerized. She couldn't see most of his face because of his beard, but his eyes were beautiful—brown, flecked with green, but they held a sadness, as well as something else she couldn't define. Mindless of all else, she continued to stare, until her father cleared his throat.

Louise blinked and tore herself away, totally ashamed of herself. She'd only kissed one man in her life, but she had at that moment been wishing her parents were elsewhere so Elliott could have kissed her now. And that was wrong.

By this time tomorrow, he would be gone. She knew he had promised to write, but writing wasn't the same as developing a personal friendship. Despite the best of intentions, she knew that soon, when he settled into his new job and his new home, that he would faithfully write, because he had promised. Then, as tended to happen, he would write less and less often, until one day the letters would simply stop. It would perhaps take a period of time, but in the end, Elliott would be one more of the countless homeless men who passed as a shadow, never to be seen again.

The thought crushed her heart like a vice.

Louise picked up the knife, and willing her hand to stop shaking, she began to cut the cake. "Who gets the first piece?"

seven

Elliott tried not to groan at the jangle of the alarm clock on the floor beside the couch. The ringing meant it was now a quarter to seven in the morning. He had fifteen minutes to wake up and prepare himself to take notes on the daily schedule, as John had instructed him to do.

His eyes burned from lack of sleep. He tried to rub it away, but the contact only made them water.

He sat up, but then flopped his head back and stared at the ceiling in the early morning light.

He didn't remember it being this way the previous night, but then he'd been so exhausted he would have slept through an earthquake.

But then, an earthquake would have been quieter. Every few hours, all night long, another train rumbled past. Not only did the trains shake the house, and therefore the couch, but the noise would have awakened the dead.

Not that he was dead, though. And with thanks to the Demchuck family, he wasn't likely to be dead soon. He hadn't realized until he'd actually begun to travel just how dangerous riding the freight trains could be. Knowing now what he didn't know then, the promise of a ticket was more than an answer to prayer.

Once more, he blinked hard, then stood, stretching his arms over his head, trying to wake himself. Slowly, he moved his head from side to side to work out the kinks in his neck, when he spotted the same jacket he'd worn the day before hanging over the back of the chair at the desk. He smiled and slipped it on and, as quietly as he could, made his way out the door. Indoor plumbing was nice, but the trip to the outhouse in the cold morning air would serve to wake him up like nothing else, including the all-night trains.

When the time came for him to pick up the phone and take notes, he was alert and ready. Exactly as he had been warned, the reception was poor. Every once in awhile he heard banging and other noises, probably made from the other people in their various sections along this rail line as they, too, listened and made their notes.

Out of curiosity, he continued to listen after the clerk in the faraway dispatch office in Kenora finished reading the schedule. Some of the men made reports that they needed rails replaced, and therefore required special equipment; others mentioned particular supplies they needed. One mentioned a problem with a switch, and then the clerk in Kenora confirmed that all things mentioned would be handled by the main office.

Overall, Elliott found the procedure fascinating. He couldn't imagine the organization or the teamwork for all those section gangs to keep the line running perfect with no downtime, yet they did. He wondered if the section foremen down this line ever got together for social activities or if their association was strictly business, at precisely seven o'clock every morning, seven days a week.

Unfortunately, he would never find out. Today, after the church service, he was leaving.

The house was quiet, although he couldn't imagine how the Demchuck family managed to sleep through the racket of the trains.

Elliott continued to sit in the chair, reading the schedule. While straining to hear, he had written as quickly as possible, not paying attention to actual content or meaning. He only wrote numbers for the sake of accuracy. Now, he could put all his notes into perspective.

It was with sadness that he read that the train he would be leaving on would be departing at half past four. He laid the paper down and counted on his fingers. Nine short hours.

He wanted to spend those nine hours with Louise, but he couldn't. Soon John would need help down the stairs and outside. Following that, they would do the morning's track inspection, which would take them to lunchtime. After lunch they would attend the Sunday worship service, and then Elliott would have less than an hour before the freight train arrived. It would stay for a short ten minutes, then depart.

Elliott suddenly froze as he found himself unconsciously stroking his beard. Now aware of what he was doing, he paid attention to what his fingers were telling him and once again touched his chin. The hair had grown soft and was no longer completely untidy, but he still didn't like it. As a barber by trade, Elliott frequently shaved other men. By the nature of his job, it was of utmost importance that he not be in need of a shave himself and that his own hair was always well trimmed.

If he shaved, he would be properly groomed for exactly one day, because he had no means to shave again until he reached his destination. Therefore, he had no alternative but to keep the beard while he traveled. When Elliott received his first paycheck, the first thing he would buy besides clothing would be a new razor.

Still, Elliott wished Louise could see him as he really was, not as an unkempt vagrant off the freight train. After he arrived at his destination, provided the job was still available, he wondered if he could get his picture taken and enclose it with a letter, telling Louise how much he missed her.

Abruptly, Elliott stood in order to rid his mind of such foolishness. He'd only had a few hours alone with Louise and known her for under two days. He could only reason that his odd attachment was in some way related to the circumstances he now found himself in.

Under normal conditions, he would have had more time to get to know her better, perhaps even court her as she deserved to be courted. However, conditions were not normal. He had no job, no assets, and no home.

His thoughts were interrupted by voices at the top of the stairs, followed by the gentle thuds of John's crutches and the heel of the cast echoing on the floor.

Without waiting to be asked, Elliott bounded up the stairs and removed the crutches from John's hands. Very slowly, one stair at a time, he guided John down while John held the handrail with one hand and supported himself on Elliott's shoulder with the other.

Once he was at the bottom and properly balanced on both crutches, John turned to Elliott. "Praise the Lord, I'll only have to do that once a day."

Louise and Mrs. Demchuck slipped behind them without speaking and scurried into the kitchen.

"Let me help you down the steps outside, and I'll wait for you."

Upon returning to the house, Elliott could already smell bacon and eggs cooking. He sat in the kitchen with John to go over the daily schedule while the women busied themselves making breakfast and setting the table.

Elliott glanced up at the clock on the wall. "According to this, we have three quarters of an hour before the next passenger train. Then we will have two and a quarter hours to do the inspection before church."

John nodded as Mrs. Demchuck and Louise set the plates on the table in front of them and poured the coffee.

Since they were in no rush, Elliott found it pure pleasure to be able to linger over their breakfast and enjoy their time together. It had been many years since he'd shared such a time with his own family, and it served as a pointed reminder of how much he missed it.

Mrs. Demchuck leaned forward on her elbows, cradling her coffee cup in her palms. "Please forgive me for asking, but we've all been so curious about you. All we know about you is that you're a barber by trade and you come from

Katona Falls in Ontario. Do you have family somewhere? Of course, we're happy that you have a job to go to. What kind of job is it that you have to travel so far?"

Elliott forced himself to smile as the unspoken question hung in the air—what was he doing riding the freight trains?

Mrs. Demchuck's question was reasonable and expected. He'd stayed with them two nights; he'd eaten their food. Mrs. Demchuck had even washed and repaired his clothing. It seemed wrong to be in this situation, being treated this way by an employee of the railroad after essentially stealing a ride on the train to get there. However, not only did they welcome him as their guest, they welcomed him as their friend.

So far, he'd successfully avoided giving them the more personal details of his life, even fooled himself into believing he could get away with it. Now, he could no longer avoid their curiosity.

He stared into his coffee cup. He would have preferred to share his hopes and dreams with these fine people, not the details of his failures.

"I'm not sure where to start. My father owned a barber-shop in Katona Falls. Our house caught fire in 1933 when I was away at university. Both my parents died in the fire."

Mrs. Demchuck lowered her cup to the table, and rested her fingers on his forearm. "Oh, Elliott. . .I'm so sorry to hear that."

"Thank you for your concern," he muttered. "It's been five years, and I still miss them, but as Christians, they're in a better place than I am." He paused, snapped his mouth shut, and cleared his throat. "I'm sorry; that came out wrong. Being here with you now is wonderful."

Louise and her mother smiled at him.

"That's okay, Elliott," Mrs. Demchuck said, patting his arm as she spoke. "I don't think our small home in the country could in any way compare to the golden gates of heaven."

John quirked up one corner of his mouth and nodded.

Immediately, Elliott relaxed, feeling better about his poor choice of wording.

Elliott cleared his throat. "Unfortunately, like so many other people, in order to cut back on expenses my parents had canceled the house insurance. I was only twenty years old and had just entered university. When they died I had to quit school. First, I couldn't find a job to support myself while I continued my schooling. Also, with our dad gone, my brother Ike needed a partner for the barbershop. So, I left school and started working with him. Since I had nowhere to stay and the house was gone, and since I'm obviously single and don't need a lot of room, we converted the storage area in the attic of the barbershop to living quarters for me. We made it into a one-bedroom suite, which suited my needs, as long as I didn't mind sharing my living room with the supplies."

His cup had long since been empty, but Elliott swirled the last few, cold drops around in the bottom and then drank them. "Ike is a few years older than I am, and he's married and has a family to support. Business for the barbershop continued to drop off, and then a couple of months ago the bank foreclosed on Ike's house. Since he needed a place to stay, he and his wife and their two children moved into the suite with me. As you can guess, it became very crowded very fast, with three adults and two children living in a one-bedroom suite above the barbershop."

They all nodded.

"We can only imagine," Mrs. Demchuck mumbled.

"By then things were so bad, we were forced to admit that the shop couldn't support all of us. Ike wasn't going to kick me out or dissolve the partnership, but then I received an answer to prayer. A letter came from an old friend, saying that if I was interested he could give me a job in a logging camp in British Columbia. He said the work would be hard, but. . ." Elliott paused to grin weakly and shrugged his shoulders. "He said that the wages were good. For now, any steady work would be good, regardless of the amount. So I wrote him back to tell him I was on my way. I'd already sold most of my furniture. I gave what was left to Ike, packed everything I owned in two suitcases, and left."

He could see their eyes widen at the thought that he could carry everything in the world he held valuable. Even he had struggled with it when it came time for him to pack. Once he'd laid everything out on the bed, he couldn't believe that everything he owned, except for a couple of pieces of furniture and a few other small items, could fit into two suitcases. As it was, he had to sell his watch in order to have enough money to pay for the bus and train tickets.

With the promise of a job, he'd considered the opportunity a new start, even though he had mixed feelings about moving away from the only place he'd ever known to live in parts unknown. In a way, he felt like one of the three little pigs out to seek his fortune. He had hoped that in the end he would liken to the little pig whose house was made of bricks.

"I bought my ticket for the bus to Ottawa, where I planned to buy a train ticket to Vancouver. The plans were that once I arrived in Vancouver, I was to contact a friend of Edward's, who would in turn contact Edward up at the logging camp, and then Edward would come and get me. But, on my way from the bus depot to the train station, a gang of men attacked me and robbed me, leaving me with nothing except the clothes on my back."

Louise gasped, and her mother covered her mouth with her hands. "That's horrible! Were you hurt?"

He rested his fingers on his neck. It didn't take much imagination to still feel the cold steel of the knife blade pressed to his throat. Fortunately, the tender spots and bruises from the beating they had given him were now healed, although his left arm still hurt when he moved it a certain way. "I wasn't badly hurt, no. But I had to decide if I should go back with nothing, knowing that Ike could barely support his own family, never mind having an extra mouth to feed. I prayed about it, and rather than take the food out of the mouths of my brother's children, I decided to carry on. And here I am. Apparently, the Lord does provide our needs, just as I was taught in Sunday school."

Silence hovered over the table and John spoke first. "That's quite a story, Elliott."

"Actually, my story is not much different than many of the men I've met along the way. Traveling like this is quite lonely. When you have time to talk to someone else in the same situation, there's an instant bond. I've always found it easy to talk to people, and this last week has been no exception. I've spoken to many men who needed the hope that you can only have with Jesus Christ in your heart. I only pray that my words have had a lasting impression on some of those men. Unfortunately, I'll never know, because I'll never see a single one of them again."

He only meant to glance up quickly, but his attention became glued to Louise. Her eyes opened wide and she appeared to be staring at a blank spot on the wall behind her father. Her eyes became strangely glassy, then she swiped her hand across them before turning to him. "We've felt that same way when we've given food or clothing to the men who pass through Pineridge. A few will listen openly to what we try to give as a message of hope, but most of them only listen to be polite because we're giving them something. We'll never know which of those we've spoken to will ever receive the message of hope and eternal salvation."

Elliott opened his mouth, about to say he understood perfectly, but a long whistle sounded in the background.

Mrs. Demchuck rose quickly. "Goodness! How the time has flown! You'd better get outside, because the train will be through in a few minutes and you have to get that inspection done quickly. We'll have a quick lunch when you're done. We don't want to be late for church."

John turned toward him. "We should try to make it across the tracks before the train arrives. We have to get the speedster out of the toolhouse."

Elliott rose, wondering if he should have been trying to help John stand. He hated to see the man struggle, but he didn't want to continuously offer help when none was required. He wanted to allow John to retain as much dignity as possible in a difficult situation. Instead, he thought about the work involved in pushing the speedster out of the toolhouse and lifting it onto the tracks. He could still feel yesterday's efforts in his back.

"I must say that speedster is a strange contraption, but it seems quite efficient for its purpose."

"Yes. But as you no doubt found the hard way, it's meant to seat only one person."

Elliott nodded. He'd barely managed to stay on the unit, and the two of them had jostled for position, both of them being quite uncomfortable for the entire time it took to travel down the tracks to do the inspection. He'd also seen the larger jigger in the toolhouse, which would have been more appropriate for more than one person. However, John had told him that it took four able-bodied men to put the jigger on the tracks every day, implying those four men were accustomed to hard work. One look at the huge jigger told him it was not a task for a man with one leg in a cast and another man whose heaviest lifting job until then consisted of occasionally lifting boxes of shampoo.

By the time they were ready to move the speedster, the train had already passed. As Elliott pulled the unit out of the toolhouse and struggled to line it up on the tracks properly, he thought about how difficult the next few hours would be.

It wasn't the track inspection he was thinking of. The track inspection was a new experience, even if it did mean a rather uncomfortable journey on the speedster. However, compared to riding the boxcars as he had been, trying to maneuver around

John on a unit that was really meant for one couldn't compare. On the bright side, as different as it was from what he was used to doing, he found the experience rather interesting.

As for attending church with the Demchucks, he very much anticipated going. He tried to think of what their service would be like and couldn't. He'd always attended the same church at home, a grand old stone building with polished oak pews and ornate stained glass windows. He couldn't imagine a church service being conducted in the small wooden building where the entire structure could have fit into his own church's Sunday school room.

Regardless of the setting, the purpose of getting together was to worship God with other believers, and that was exactly what he planned to do. While trying to imagine the order of the service, he wondered if Louise would be playing the organ. Part of him hoped she would, because he wanted to hear her play, but part of him didn't. He didn't want to participate with her from across the room, no matter how small he knew it would be. He wanted to worship God with her at his side.

Suddenly, the reason for his apprehension about leaving hit him with the force of a tornado.

The reason he didn't want to leave was because he didn't want to say good-bye to Louise.

eight

Louise stood at the window, watching her father and Elliott start off down the track on the speedster.

"It was good of him to stay one more day, wasn't it?" her mother said from behind her.

"He'll get to the coast faster with a ticket, even leaving one day later," Louise muttered, continuing to stare down the track, even though the men had disappeared from sight.

"Did you tell him he doesn't need to know the address, just Pineridge?"

Louise spun around so quickly her skirt billowed around her knees. "Mama!"

Her mother didn't even have the grace to blush. Fortunately, she didn't comment further.

"I think we should do the dishes and make lunch; then I'll change into my good dress." Without needing instructions, Louise pushed the plates to the side, took the basin down from its hook on the wall, carried it to the cookstove, and filled it with warm water.

"For lunch, we're going to use the rest of yesterday's roast beef for sandwiches. The bread should be ready to come out of the oven in a few minutes. I was also thinking we might make some donuts for dessert."

Louise nearly dropped the basin of water on the floor. "Dessert? At lunchtime? And donuts? Before church? Doesn't that take too long?"

This time, it gave Louise great satisfaction to see her mother's cheeks darken.

"Hush, Girl. We'll have time if we hurry. You carry that water, and I'll go get the flour and sugar out of the cellar."

Louise chatted very little with her mother as they worked to complete their tasks. The long periods of silence allowed her to think. She could tell her mother liked Elliott. She couldn't help but like him, too. However, Louise suspected there was more to her mother's words than had been said aloud. She deemed this was her mother's unstated approval to keep in contact with him.

Aside from Mr. Farley's son Johnathan and William McSorbin, one of the local farmer's sons, there were no other young men in Pineridge. The only times she had opportunity to meet other young men her age was when their family traveled to Winnipeg every month and stayed at the homes of friends or relatives in the city.

So far, she had not met anyone specifically to her liking beyond a simple friendship. However, at nearly twenty years of age, it was time for her to start thinking of her future and getting married. Louise would have liked to take the time to see if Elliott could have been that special man God had chosen for her, but she would never know. Later that day, he would be gone and living over a thousand miles away.

Just as she finished frying the last donut, she heard the squeal of metal wheels on the track in front of the house.

"They're back, Mama!"

"Quickly, Louise. Go change your dress now, and I'll finish putting the donuts on a plate."

Obediently, Louise ran up the stairs and quickly selected her favorite dress and, along with it, a hat with lace bows that her mother had made to match her dress. She picked up the hand mirror from atop her dresser, appraised herself quickly, adjusted one of the bows, returned the hat to the dresser until it was time to go, and ran back downstairs.

Since the men had not yet come inside the house, Louise slipped her apron back on to protect her good dress and poured the coffee into the cups already on the table.

Behind her, the door closed with a bang. "Wow. Something smells great!"

"Mama made donuts."

Elliott's eyebrows raised, and one hand settled on his stomach. "Homemade donuts? Wow."

Louise smiled. "You've never had homemade donuts?"

"Never."

"Mama makes the best donuts in Pineridge." She beamed.

"Hush, Louise. You can make them just as well as I can."

Across the table, Elliott remained standing while her papa inched his way toward his chair and slowly began to lower himself, leaning on the crutches for support with one hand and steadying himself with his other palm on the tabletop. "I must be getting old. I'm so tired, and we haven't even had lunch."

Without warning, the crutches slipped on the linoleum. Her father's eyes widened as his unsupported weight on the edge of the table caused it to shudder, and suddenly, as his side of the table started to go down, the other end started to go up.

In her mind, Louise pictured all their dishes and their lunch, hot coffee and all, flying through the air, and her father crashing to the floor. She sucked in a deep breath to scream, but before a sound came out, Elliott pushed all his weight on his corner of the table to steady it. With the table held firm, her father regained his balance, half leaning and half hanging onto the edge of the table.

The dishes clattered and settled. Some dribbles of coffee ran over the surface of the table, but the cups all remained upright.

Her father dropped himself into the chair and covered his face with his hands. "I'm sorry, Anna. You can't believe how difficult this is."

Her mother turned away and busily tucked the sandwiches back into good order. "Hush, John. I know it's hard. The nurse told me when we left you for the night that little mishaps would happen, and she was right. It will take time to become accustomed to moving around on crutches, plus she said your balance will be off. Now, everybody, let's eat. We don't want to be late for church."

This time, Elliott prayed over the food, and because of the late hour, they ate more quickly than at breakfast.

"Thank you for a wonderful lunch, Mrs. Demchuck."

"Hush, Elliott. I haven't done all this by myself. Louise has done more than her share. Louise is a very good cook, isn't she?"

Louise stiffened in her chair. "Mama!" she hissed quietly, then quickly turned to force a toothy smile at Elliott.

He blinked twice and stared back. "Yes, she certainly is. I've never in my life eaten so well as these last two days."

Thankfully, instead of saying more, her mother rose. "If you'll excuse me, I must change my dress before church. John, I've left a clean shirt for you by the washbasin, and Elliott, I've taken a few tucks in one of John's shirts, so you can also have something to wear, although I'm afraid your own trousers will have to do."

"Thank you, Mrs. Demchuck. I appreciate everything you've done for me more than words can say."

"And we appreciate all you've done for us as well. Now let's hurry, or we'll be late."

Louise ran upstairs to fetch her hat, but before she set it on her head, she ran her brush through her hair to fix it and applied a thin coat of lipstick to her lips. She'd never much cared for such things, but today she wanted to look her best.

She waited in the living room with her mama while the men washed and changed their shirts. Even though it wasn't far, walking down the dirt road on crutches would be too difficult for her father; so she and her mama walked to the church and Elliott drove her father with the car, since only three people could fit inside.

"Mama, you can go join Papa and Elliott. I have to talk to Mildred for a minute."

Before her mother could protest, she ran off to speak to her friend, then returned as quickly as she could to be with her family.

Rather than stand around to talk, they escorted her father up the two steps and helped him take a seat inside where he could talk to people who were curious about his cast and his accident.

When the service began, Pastor Galbraith welcomed all present. He extended a special welcome to her father for coming in spite of the cast and then reviewed the community announcements.

Mildred walked to the organ, and the congregation stood.

"Louise," her mother whispered in her ear, "why is Mildred playing the organ?"

Louise turned to whisper back. "I asked her to trade with me. I wanted to sit in the congregation today."

Her mother's one raised eyebrow told her that she knew it was a specific visitor in the congregation with whom she wanted to sit. Ignoring her mother's telltale smirk, Louise flipped through the hymnal to the correct page and began to sing with the congregation.

She nearly choked on her words when Elliott began to sing beside her. Not only did he sing in a lovely baritone, but he sang in perfect flowing harmony for every song. The rich blend of his voice, combined with the deep bass of Mr. Sabinski, the only other man in the congregation who could also sing a harmony, profoundly affected everyone present during the time they worshiped the Lord with their songs.

Elliott sat with rapt attention for the entire length of the sermon and mumbled an enthusiastic "amen" each time Pastor Galbraith made a good point.

After the close of the service, many people approached them to talk, first, because having a visitor to their small congregation in the country was rare, but mostly, Louise suspected, it was because Elliott's fine singing had created a stir.

Mildred was the first person to approach him. "Was that

you singing like that? Praise the Lord for your lovely voice!"

In the bright sunlight, Louise could see the color of Elliott's checks darken, even beneath the beard.

"I love to sing, especially for the Lord on Sunday."

"I hope your home church has a choir, and that you are in it."

"Yes, I am. I'm also a member of a barbershop quartet, which is a lot of fun. Actually, I get teased a lot about that, because I really am a barber."

He smiled fully, showing a beautiful set of teeth, in addition to his beautiful smile. It made Louise long to see that same smile more often, but she felt the minutes ticking away, reminding her that their time together was running out.

As much as she didn't want him to go, she didn't want him to miss the train, either. "Elliott, you stay here with my friends. I'm going to find Papa and see if he's ready to go. I'll tell him you'll be at the car shortly, but I know it will take him longer to get there than you."

His answering smile made her foolish heart flutter. Before he noticed that she was acting strange, Louise walked away, in search of her parents.

Since she didn't see them outside talking to anyone, Louise walked back into the church. Not finding them there either, she stood still and crossed her arms, wondering where they could have gone. Then, she heard what sounded like her father's voice coming from the doorway leading to the Sunday school classroom.

Because she was in the Lord's house, Louise didn't call out to them. Instead she approached them, meaning to speak to them at a respectful volume.

Her feet skidded to a halt on the polished wood floor when she heard her father mention Elliott's name.

"John! Are you serious?" she heard her mother whisper to her father. Even though she couldn't see her mother's face, Louise well imagined her expression. Surely she would be standing with her arms crossed and her head tilted to one side. Any second, Louise expected to hear the tapping of her mother's shoe on the hard floor.

Her papa replied, his voice also hushed. "I know what you're thinking, Anna, but listen to me. I know he doesn't know what he's doing. I'm not sure that he's very mechanically minded, but you should have seen him out there. He has a real eye for detail. More so, he's humble, and he's teachable. He's young, but he's an honorable man, and that combination makes him more suitable than anyone could ever be."

"Do you know what you're asking him to do?"

"I'm not asking him to turn down the other job. He told me that he doesn't have a specific starting date; his friend's letter said whenever he got there. I want to ask him if he could get in touch with his friend and ask if the job would still be his in eight weeks. If he has to go, I'll certainly understand, but I really believe the Lord has placed Elliott in our path at this time for a reason."

"I don't know, John."

"I've prayed about it, and I have my answer. It's up to Elliott now."

"You'd better ask him quickly, then. Doesn't the train leave soon? You're not giving him much time to think about it. This is a big decision for him. And what about Louise?"

"What about her? I don't think it will be that much more work for her if we have to feed an extra person for a couple of months."

"You don't understand. Louise has taken a shine to him. And rightly so—he seems to be a fine young man. But this presents a problem."

"How so? I believe that he feels the same way about her, so why would that be a bad thing?"

"As her parents, we must make sure they aren't left open to temptation. But more than that. What about when he leaves? She's my daughter, and I don't want her to be hurt."

"Anna, she's not a little girl. She's nearly twenty years old, old enough to be married. Nothing will happen if she knows he'll be leaving again."

"I don't know. . . ."

"She's a sensible girl, and you said it yourself; Elliott is an honorable young man. Come on. We have to find him so I can take him aside and talk."

Louise didn't need to hear anymore. As fast as her feet would go without taking the chance of making noise on the hardwood floor, she hurried across the room. Once outside, she ran the rest of the way.

She found Elliott alone, leaning against the flagpole. He straightened as soon as he saw her coming.

"There you are. I was wondering where you went and what was taking you so long. I wanted to talk to you about something privately."

Louise's throat tightened. She didn't know what to think. Of course, she would have loved him to stay so she could get to know him better, but if that meant risking his job, then such thinking was selfish. "There's something I have to tell you, too."

"Please, let me go first; this is difficult. I'll be leaving soon, and this is my last chance."

"But—"

He held up his palms to silence her. "No, please, let me finish. This is difficult. I know I've said I would write, but I should have asked you first if you would like to exchange letters with me, rather than expecting you would want to. For my lack of manners, I apologize."

"Elliott, listen to me." Quickly, she turned her head from side to side to make sure her parents hadn't caught up to her yet. "We may not be exchanging letters."

"Oh. I'm sorry. I should have realized there was already someone else in your heart. Now if you'll excuse me—"

"Hush, Elliott," she whispered and reached forward to

touch his sleeve, halting him in his tracks. "It's not that. I heard Mama and Papa talking. Papa is going to ask if you'll stay here and be his lead hand until he's out of the cast and back to work."

"Lead hand? But I know nothing of maintaining the track other than what little your father told me over the last two days."

Louise nodded so fast her hat wobbled on her head. She reached up with her free hand to straighten it and kept talking. "I know. I'm only repeating what I heard. He trusts you."

"Well. . .I'm honored. I don't know what to say."

"Of course, he knows you have another job, but he says from the sound of it, you don't have a specific start date."

"I'm not entirely sure of that until either I get there to speak to Edward or somehow find a way to get a letter to him."

She glanced behind her to see her parents advancing slowly.

"I probably shouldn't have told you, but I couldn't help myself."

One side of his mouth quirked up. "I'm glad you did. Today while we were out, your father asked me some rather strange questions. I thought I had done something wrong, yet he assured me that wasn't the case. It all makes sense now."

"What are you going to do?"

"There's only one thing I can do. I have to think about it and pray. But I suppose I shouldn't do that until your father talks to me and gives me all the details and tells me all my options."

Once again, Elliott got the car to drive her father the short distance home, leaving Louise to walk with her mother.

"Let's walk slowly. Your father has something to talk to Elliott about, and they may be awhile."

Louise inhaled deeply, then let all the air out in a whoosh. She couldn't look at her mother as she spoke. "I know. I'm sorry, Mama, but I heard you and Papa talking."

"Did you tell Elliott?"

"Yes. I'm sorry."

"It's okay. You've never been good at keeping secrets. I suppose it's foolish of me to expect that you could start now."

Louise didn't know what to say, so she said nothing.

When they arrived at the house, instead of joining the men in the living room, they went in through the back door and immediately started making preparations for dinner. Louise brought a roast pork out of the outdoor cellar, and they peeled potatoes to tuck inside the roaster before it went into the oven.

Although she could hear the murmur of their voices, Louise couldn't hear their actual words from where she was. After a rather lengthy conversation, a long silence followed. Louise suspected that they were praying for wisdom for Elliott's decision.

Even though he'd met with hard times, Elliott Endicott truly was an honorable and godly man. One day, he would make some lucky woman a wonderful husband.

She nearly dropped the potato onto the floor, startled with pangs of jealousy for a woman who so far didn't exist.

Louise and her mother continued to make dinner, not knowing if Elliott would be staying or leaving with the passenger train that was due shortly. Louise didn't want to think about it, so she struggled to think of other things while she did the worst job she'd ever done of slicing carrots.

The carrot she'd been peeling dropped to the floor when her father and Elliott entered the kitchen.

"Anna, Louise. I hope you're setting a fourth plate at the table. Elliott has agreed to be my lead hand for eight weeks."

"That's wonderful!" Louise and her mother said in unison.

Louise wanted to run to Elliott and throw her arms around him but couldn't do so in front of her parents, especially after what she'd heard them discussing about watching her interaction with Elliott during the time he was there.

"We're going to name his position officially as lead hand, but really his duties will be mine, and he will act as substitute section foreman. For at least the first few weeks, after the daytime work with the section men is done, I'll have to teach Elliott the rest of the job in the evenings, since that is the only way he can be properly trained. Because of that, he can't be staying in the bunkhouse with the section men. We've decided that he's going to continue sleeping here on the couch. This way he can take the scheduling call every morning at seven, as well and he'll be here for me when I need help."

Louise clasped her hands together. "I'm so glad, Elliott! And that means you'll be making a good salary, too."

"Until he gets his first paycheck, he's going to borrow whatever of mine he needs. Anna, you're going to have to help him, since I can't. In fact, I think I'm going to go lie down on the couch until dinner is ready."

Louise stood in silence as her father hobbled into the living room.

Her mother wiped her hands on her apron as she spoke. "I'm going to enjoy having you here, Elliott. I can show you where everything is now that dinner is cooking and Louise is doing the vegetables. What's the first thing you want to see?"

Elliott ran his hand over his chin and smiled from ear to ear. "A razor."

nine

Louise didn't know which was less proper, to go into the living room where her father was trying to sleep or to stay in the kitchen and work with her mother while Elliott shaved.

She'd occasionally been in the kitchen when her father had shaved but only when it couldn't be avoided. Besides, her father was family, which allowed them to bend the rules of propriety somewhat.

Elliott wasn't family. He could have been loosely considered family as a Christian brother, but already in her heart, he was much more than that. She'd become quite fond of him, but that didn't mean she wanted to watch him shave. It would almost be like. . .Elliott watching her pluck her eyebrows.

As nice as the houses were that the railroad provided to the families of the section foremen, their house was small. Besides the living and dining rooms or the kitchen, her only option would be to go upstairs to her bedroom where she had nothing to do. She couldn't do that, because she had plenty of work in the kitchen helping her mother prepare dinner. She still had to finish preparing the carrots and potatoes, and they still hadn't finished cleaning up the extra mess from making the donuts.

Mostly, going up to her bedroom would be cowardly.

She finished peeling and slicing the carrots while Elliott pumped some water into the kettle and placed it on the cookstove.

As he continued to gather up the shaving supplies, Louise couldn't help but watch him out of the corner of her eye. She wondered if a professional barber would shave differently than her father.

He leaned close to the mirror and ran his fingers through the beard. "May I trouble you for some scissors? My whiskers are too long for the razor."

Her mother left the room and returned with her sewing scissors, which Louise knew were the best scissors in the house. He stared at them as her mother placed them in his palm.

"I know they're not like the barber scissors you're used to, but that's what I use to cut John's hair."

Louise bit her lip when she saw the slight movement of Elliott cringing. Her mother returned to the cookstove, and without speaking, Elliott leaned close to the mirror and snipped away as much length as he could. He then laid the scissors on the table beside the basin and poured a little water into the shaving mug, whipped up the soap into a fluffy lather, and set it aside.

He smiled as he pulled the blade of her father's razor out of its slot in the handle, then gently ran his thumb along the cutting edge. "I suspect this will have to be sharpened when I'm done. Do you know where John keeps his strop?"

"If it's not there, then I'm not sure. I'll ask him later."

From where she stood, even though his back was to her, Louise could see his face in the mirror. She watched as Elliott patted his face with warm water, then brushed on a thick layer of lather. Slowly, and in small sections, he scraped the razor along his cheeks and under his chin, but she couldn't watch as he shaved under his nose.

When he was done, he bent at the waist and rinsed his face with the water in the basin, then stood as he patted his cheeks dry with the towel.

Just as he was about to remove the towel from his face, their gazes met in the mirror. Elliott froze, his eyes widened, and Louise couldn't force herself to look away. Almost in slow motion, he turned, not lowering the towel from his face.

When he spoke, not only was his voice muffled from speaking through the towel, but there was also a husky quality Louise had not heard before.

"I don't want you to be disappointed, but nothing is going to change me now. This is what I really look like."

Slowly, he lowered the towel from his face. Instead of his smile being warm and friendly, it looked like he was trying too hard to smile for a photograph.

His eyes were the same, but everything else seemed different. Even his nose without the mustache beneath it seemed somehow changed, and his hair appeared lighter than before, although that didn't make sense.

While she wouldn't have called him handsome, he was by no means ugly. Without the beard, all his features seemed thinner. His cheekbones were more prominent and his nose seemed longer. His forced smile showed thin lines beside his mouth, although she suspected they would fill out after her mother's good cooking put more meat on his bones.

She'd never paid notice to a man's chin before, but even with his thin features, he had a strong jawline. Though it was forced, he had a lovely smile without all the dark hair surrounding his mouth.

Louise grasped both sides of her skirt, smiled, and curtsied. "Pleased to meet you, Mr. Endicott. Although I'm sure we've met before."

Something in his smile changed. The lines softened and the start of crow's-feet appeared at the corners of his eyes, and this time, a genuine smile lit his face. He rested one arm in front of his stomach with the towel still clutched in his hand and slid the other behind him as he bowed politely. "Ma'am."

Louise lifted both hands to her mouth. "Ma'am? Didn't you promise not to say that?"

"I only promised your mother. Now I think I should clean up the mess I've made, and you'd better get finished with those carrots before your mother becomes angry with me for distracting you."

❧

After waiting for John to sit first, Elliott sank onto the couch.

He'd never been so tired in his life. Beyond the overtiredness due to the lack of sleep while riding the freight trains, this was different. This was simple and complete exhaustion. He hurt all over. Even his hair hurt. Well, maybe not his hair, but certainly everything else did. He had sore muscles where he didn't know he had muscles.

John had told him that it took four men to lift the jigger, although it could be done in a struggle with three. He should have put this into perspective. John moved the smaller speedster with little effort. Doing the same thing, Elliott felt like he'd put his back out and strained every muscle in his entire body.

The heavy-duty construction of the recessed handles used to move the jigger also should have given him a hint of the physical exertion required. Once they actually started to lift the heavy unit, without John being able to help, Elliott didn't think he and the other two section men were going to manage. After much struggle, they finally did wrestle the beast onto the tracks, although he didn't know how.

Fortunately, it was not quite as difficult to get it off the tracks as to put it on.

This was a daily part of the job.

Compared to him, the other two men possessed the strength of Samson—before the haircut.

Since they were missing an experienced man, he'd pitched in to work replacing ties, just as the regular lead hand would have done, rather than just stand by and supervise. Even though Frank and Henry were older than him by ten years, so far it appeared that they had accepted his position of leadership without question. Just to be safe, John had warned him not to tell them of his inexperience or how he'd come to arrive there until he felt confident of his ability to lead the section gang without John present.

Hopefully, soon he would know what he was supposed to be doing beyond the basics, and the unaccustomed demands on him physically would build his strength quickly. Until he could perform the duties of the section foreman without assistance, every evening would be spent with John teaching him what was involved in maintaining thirty miles of parallel railroad tracks.

Except, Elliott didn't know if he'd be able to stay awake.

If he had been at home, he would have ignored the rest of the world, ignored his aches and pains, ignored everything going on around him, and crawled into his bed. He wouldn't even have eaten dinner, because he was more exhausted than he was hungry. But here, he and John and Mrs. Demchuck were sitting on his bed.

The only person missing was Louise. According to her mother, Louise had gone on her bicycle to a nearby farm and had not yet returned.

He'd thought of her often during the day. Whenever they'd finished removing a tie, sliding in a new one, then driving in the spikes to hold the new one in place, they could take a short break until the next train passed. After a short time, they would pack their tools and the tie they'd removed and move to the next location he and John had marked on the weekend. In those slower moments, his thoughts drifted to Louise.

Now, when the bright spot of his long, hard day would have been seeing her, she wasn't at home. He thought it odd that she would run such an errand and be late for dinnertime, but Mrs. Demchuck had told him that they'd unexpectedly run out of eggs because they had been doing more baking during the day. Louise was due back any minute, and upon her return, they would serve dinner.

Elliott let his eyes close as he wondered what delectable treat they had made for dessert today. He'd never eaten like this in his life. He suspected that after the eight weeks were up, John's cast was removed, and he would be on his way, he never would eat like this again.

He sighed deeply, allowing himself to relax a little more, without opening his eyes. Louise's honey cake was great, but the donuts were better. He'd never tasted anything like them.

But then the strawberry and rhubarb pie they'd made yesterday at dinnertime had been great, too. Now that he thought about it, before he and John had left that morning, Mrs. Demchuck had mentioned during breakfast that they were going to make a walnut cake and how important it was that they had fresh eggs. He didn't know that an egg being laid a few days ago versus that morning would make a big difference in a cake, but he chose not to voice his opinion. After all, she knew all about delicious baked goods, and he knew nothing except that Mrs. Demchuck and Louise cooked food like he'd never had in his life.

Elliott sank deeper into the couch, and his head flopped over to the side. If they kept this up, he might get very spoiled, very fast.

The murmur of John and Mrs. Demchuck's voices droned on, and a Glenn Miller tune came on the radio. In the background, he heard a small bang but ignored it. He would open his eyes in just a minute. . . .

"Elliott? Are you sleeping?"

His eyes sprang open and he sat up with a jolt. With a slight shake of his head, the world came into focus and, with it, the sight of Louise standing above him.

Elliott rubbed his eyes. "I'm sorry. I guess I was more tired than I thought. Please forgive me for being so rude."

He thought his heart was pounding from being startled, but it only seemed to get worse with Louise hovering above him.

"That's okay. I know you're tired. I didn't think this would take so long. Apparently, you created quite a stir in church yesterday. Everyone is talking about the stranger with the lovely tenor voice in our midst. I had nearly made it out of the McSorbins' house when Dorothy started asking about you. Do you remember her? She wore a hat with a yellow ribbon to church."

He remembered meeting a number of young women yesterday, but no one particularly stuck out in his mind. He had accompanied Louise, and since at the time he'd thought he would only have a few hours left with her, he hadn't paid attention to much else, especially other young ladies. "I don't really remember. Sorry."

She rested her fingertips on his shoulder as she spoke, and his heart continued to beat far too fast. "Don't worry. I told her simply that you were a friend of the family and that as a special favor, you were going to be staying on as part of the section gang until Papa's cast is removed."

His throat constricted. He hadn't yet thought about what his relationship to Louise or her family was to be. Considering the short amount of time he had known them, he thought it an honor to be counted as their friend. However, he wasn't sure that friendship with Louise was exactly what he wanted.

At twenty-five years of age, it was time for him to settle down—to find a wife and raise a family. So far, he had not met a woman who interested him in such a manner. Until now. In only a few days, he'd become quite fond of Louise. He couldn't stop thinking about her, to the point of wondering if, as they got to know each other better, their association could go past friendship and perhaps into a courtship.

Suddenly, her fingers moved off his shoulder, and Louise hurried into the kitchen.

Mrs. Demchuck followed Louise, but Elliott remained seated. He was in no position to think of courting Louise or any young woman. The only reason he had a job for the moment was because her father had given it to him, not because he deserved it, neither had he earned it. John had only given him this job because John was desperate, and Elliott had happened to be in the right place at the right time, by God's timing. This job was temporary. He still didn't know for sure that the job promised to him at the logging camp would come to pass, which was the main reason he'd accepted John's offer.

Under such circumstances, he had no security to offer a

woman, especially Louise. Her father possessed the most secure income, if not the largest, in the community. Even the business owners in town were at the whim of the economy. Elliott, on the other hand, had no real permanent job and no assets. He didn't even have a home to live in, rented or otherwise. For now, only because God had provided, his home was the couch in the Demchucks' living room.

If Louise wanted to think of him as a friend, and friend only, she obviously had more sense than he did.

Friends, it would be, and it would never be any other way.

And then, in eight short weeks, he would be gone.

"Papa! Elliott! Dinner is ready! Come into the kitchen."

Elliott pushed himself up, offered his hand to John, and accompanied him into the kitchen.

ಶಿ

Louise removed the basins from their hooks on the wall and set them on the table while her mother filled the kettle to heat the water to wash the dishes. Today was Louise's turn to dry and put everything away in the hutch on the other side of the kitchen. Usually she preferred to wash, but today, she had changed her mind.

She hadn't thought about it before, but every time she walked back and forth from the table to the hutch to put the clean dishes away she could look through the doorway between the kitchen and dining room and watch Elliott and her father sitting at the desk.

She didn't mean to eavesdrop, but she couldn't help looking every time she walked past.

As they had every other time the two men sat together at the desk, Elliott sat to the left with his left leg sticking out to the side, her father to the right with his casted right leg extended on the outside of the desk. Beneath the small desk, Elliott's right leg and her father's left almost pressed together as they sat side by side.

She slowed her pace every time she walked past the opening.

At varying times, Elliott nodded as her father talked while referring to different papers on the desk. Once it appeared her father had attempted to draw a picture and pointed to it as he explained something.

Every time Louise walked past, she noticed Elliott's posture sagged a wee bit more and he sat a little less upright. From behind as she walked back and forth, often she could see his complete profile as the two men faced each other. Elliott's eyes progressively became less and less bright, and his expression began to dull from the combination of exhaustion and information overload.

Her mother's voice from behind her nearly made her drop the plate from her hands.

"Louise, if you want to put the plates and cups away one at a time, that's fine with me. But if you think you are going to continue walking back and forth with every single piece of cutlery, you had better think again."

Her cheeks burned as she hurried to the hutch, tucked the plate onto the stack, and shuffled back to the table, where she picked up a handful of the clean cutlery. Louise opened her mouth, intending to defend herself, but her words caught in her throat. Her mother was nibbling on her lower lip in an attempt not to laugh.

"It's not funny, Mama. He's almost falling asleep in the chair and Papa is still talking. You saw him at the dinner table. I was surprised he didn't nod off while we were eating."

Her mother's grin faded. "Of course, you're right. We know he's not used to this pace or this much work. Perhaps it's a good thing that cake didn't make it into the oven until so late. If it's done, this is a good reason to interrupt them."

Louise nearly ran across the room as she dried the handful of cutlery and closed the drawer.

"The walnut cake does smell done. Do you remember what time we put it in the oven?"

"No, I only remember that it was when we called Elliott

and your papa for dinner and that it was late."

Louise picked up the pot holders and opened the oven to remove the cake. As the heavy door swung open to the right, she stepped to the left to avoid the rush of heat. She bent at the waist to examine the cake before lifting it out. Since it was nicely rounded in the center, she reached inside, lifted the cake out, and set it on the flat surface of the cookstove. Gently, she pressed her finger into the center of the cake and smiled when the indent she made bounced back. "It's done, Mama." Today, she would not wait for the cake to cool before she cut it.

She walked to the doorway between the kitchen and dining room and stopped. "Elliott? Papa? The cake is done. Would you like to stop and have a piece?"

Her father raised his arms over his head and stretched his back, while Elliott arched his shoulders and moved slightly from side to side. Her father then pushed the papers to the back of the desk and laid down his pen. "I think that's enough for one night anyway. Let's have that cake, and maybe we will call it an early night."

Without her father being able to see him, Elliott looked directly into her eyes, mouthed a thank-you, and stood. Louise knew she had done the right thing.

"I can hardly wait to taste that cake. It's been teasing me as it cooked. If you keep this up, by the time eight weeks go by, I'm afraid I may become very spoiled and very fat."

Louise smiled. Not that she wanted to make him fat, but he did need to put on more weight for his height. "Nonsense. Now come and have a piece of cake. Mama is cutting it now. It's my favorite recipe, and it's wonderful when it's warm."

ten

"Good-bye, Papa! We'll be back in time for dinner."

"This will be a good time to catch up on my reading. Have fun shopping."

Louise waved to her father, who was standing on his crutches in the doorway and watching Elliott back the car out of the garage. Her mother gave him a quick peck on the cheek as she moved around him. Louise and her mother hurried to the car and got in while Elliott closed the garage door, and they were on their way.

"I can't say how much I appreciate this, Mrs. Demchuck."

"Nonsense. I simply don't have time to have to wash the same clothes so often."

Louise smiled at Elliott's grace in not saying more. All week long they had no choice but to have him wear the only set of clothes he'd arrived with, and when they became soiled, her mama had loaned him some of her father's clothes, which fit him poorly. A shopping trip was exactly what he needed to purchase some shirts and trousers of his own, in addition to a few personal items.

They hadn't discussed it, but she was perfectly aware that Elliott was not comfortable borrowing her father's personal things, but he had no choice. Unfortunately, because he'd only worked for the railroad for a week he'd missed the pay period. Because of that, her parents offered to give him enough money to cover a few necessities. Elliott had been awkward about accepting their money. He'd made it clear that this was strictly a loan which he would repay promptly out of his first paycheck.

"When I went to Nick's store, I saw a few shirts and other

items that I could have purchased instead of going all the way into Beauséjour."

"Hush, Elliott. Nick's prices for clothing are outrageous. Why, the same shirt that he charges a dollar and a quarter for, we can get in Beauséjour for a dollar. We could probably get it for ninety-five cents in Winnipeg, but that would involve making arrangements to stay overnight, as it's simply too far to do in a day. Besides, since you haven't worked for the railroad long enough, you're not entitled to free rail passes, as we are. We shop at Nick's store on the odd weeks we don't go to Winnipeg. His food items are reasonable, but he charges far too much for the clothing and sundries."

"Yes, I had noticed that much of his merchandise was fairly high priced."

Elliott slowed the car, and Louise almost asked what he was doing when a doe stepped out onto the road. However, the noise from the car frightened it, and it disappeared back into the trees quickly.

Elliott turned his head to stare into the bush where the deer had disappeared as he drove past, then once again faced forward. "That was beautiful. I don't see a lot of wild animals in Katona Falls. I suppose that out here you must see a lot of wild animals."

"Yes. Sometimes I think I see more animals than people in Pineridge because very few people ever come off the trains. We're so far away from a city that even the iceman won't come by. I suppose you've noticed we don't have an icebox."

He smiled as he drove, glancing only quickly toward her before returning his attention to the dirt road ahead of him and all its hazards. "Yes, I did notice that. I suppose that's why you don't have a telephone, either."

"I guess you noticed that the phone is only connected to the other section houses, and the district office."

"Yes, I did notice that. This area is very remote. Do animals ever come right into the town of Pineridge? It's not what I'd call a bustling metropolis."

Louise giggled and told Elliott about the time a family of skunks made themselves at home under the porch at Mr. Tolson's repair shop and the ensuing disaster trying to remove them once their nest was discovered. Every drop of tomato juice had been purchased from Mr. Sabinski's store that day.

They were still laughing when they finally arrived at the main street of Beauséjour. They parked the car near the first general store on Park Avenue, then walked to the smaller store on Second Street for a better selection of the cotton yarn her mother needed to make sweaters to give away to the homeless men who passed through. Her mother made Elliott stand next to the bin of yarn while she selected her colors, which told Louise without words that the next sweater her mama made would be for Elliott.

Next they took Elliott through the few stores in town. He graciously accepted her mama's assistance in choosing the best styles and colors for the trousers and shirts he picked, although they allowed him the privacy to select his more personal clothing items alone.

Once Elliott paid for his selections, they walked to the drugstore. He held the door open for them to enter, but when Louise stepped inside, her mama stopped.

"I have a list of things to get. I'll meet you back here."

Without waiting for Louise to respond, her mama turned on her heels and nearly ran down the walk.

Louise looked up to see Elliott standing beside her, frozen, his mouth open and one finger in the air.

She pressed her hand to her mouth to muffle her sudden case of the giggles, but she couldn't control herself.

"You'll have to excuse Mama," she said between her fingers. "We've never been shopping without Papa before, since he has to drive us. I heard them talking, and he gave her some extra money to spend. She's very excited. She's never been shopping alone before."

"I suppose this will give me more time to buy what I need, then. Do you want to come with me, or do you have a special list, too?"

Louise smiled. She'd never wanted anything more. "Mama has the list, so I'll go with you."

Slowly, she directed him through the store to the men's area, where he began to browse through the selection of razors and other men's toiletries.

While Elliott compared the different razor handles without speaking, Louise stepped closer to him so other shoppers couldn't hear her words.

"I suppose this is all very strange for you."

He let out a very humorless laugh. "You have no idea. I feel like I'm starting all over again, and in a way, I suppose I am."

"Did you lose everything?"

"What I didn't sell before I left, I more or less gave to my brother and his family. Except for stuff like my photo album and a few smaller but heavier items, I packed everything I had left into my suitcases and took it with me. I was counting on things working out enough to the point where it would be a permanent move out of Katona Falls. When I was robbed, it all happened so fast. I certainly didn't expect something like that to happen so close to home. There were at least five men in the group who attacked me. I thought people only got mugged in Toronto."

Louise shook her head. "These modern times are frightening, especially with so many desperate people out there. I've always felt safe around here, but I suppose that will change someday. The important thing is that you weren't hurt. . .or worse."

He raised his hand to his throat, then quickly dropped it to his side as he turned to select a comb. "I suppose it's better to be a live coward than a dead hero." He turned to her as quickly as he'd just turned away. "I've wondered over and over what lesson there was in being robbed like that, and I just can't figure it out. I like to think that I choose my battles intelligently. I believe in my heart I did the right thing by not fighting back because I was badly outnumbered. Plus, they had a weapon and I didn't. The contents of those two suitcases were basically all I had left, but they were not worth fighting impossible odds. I don't think anything but my clothes would be of much value to anyone. Still, I hope that somewhere, someone is reading my Bible and thinking of what the words say, although I suspect that it's just been thrown in a trash bin somewhere. In the end God provided for me, although it's in a way I could never have imagined in my wildest dreams—or nightmares. I don't know what would have happened to me without you and your family."

Louise's throat tightened. She couldn't believe they were having such a conversation beside the men's deodorants. "We would have done the same for anyone in your situation. It's what we feel the Lord has called us to do as a family. Now let's talk about something else. Shopping is supposed to be fun."

His hesitant smile made Louise's foolish heart flutter. "I've never considered shopping fun. I buy what I need and go home."

At the same time, they heard her mother approaching and turned in unison. Her mama's arms were filled with bags, making Louise shake her head and wonder what wonderful bargains she'd found this shopping trip, especially without her papa present to temper her choices.

Louise lowered her voice to a whisper. "Mama normally considers shopping an adventure, today even more so."

Her mother joined them, smiling from ear to ear. "I never knew they carried yarn here. And such a good price! I've never seen these prices, not even in Winnipeg. And such a fine quality cotton! It will take me until Christmas to knit all this, but I look forward to it. Here, Elliott. You can carry these bags for me." Without waiting for him to respond, she emptied everything she carried into Elliott's arms, only retaining her purse. "Have you finished here? I still have a few things left to buy, and we have to be home for dinner. It's a long drive home."

"I've made my selections, but I don't know where they are under everything I'm carrying."

Her mama led Elliott to the counter, where Louise helped him put all the bags down neatly. He then paid for his own items, and they continued on.

Every time they stopped at another store and her mama made another purchase, Elliott ended up with more packages to carry. He never complained, even though Louise didn't know how he managed to hold everything without dropping something. She did notice his sigh of relief when her mama suggested they return to the car before they continued with the last of their shopping, which was for groceries.

The entire time they were in the grocery store, instead of carrying it or walking to the counter, her mama handed everything to Elliott, who made many trips to pile everything on the counter as they shopped. The entire time, Elliott behaved as a perfect gentleman, being very good-natured and teasing her mama that at least he didn't have to carry everything at once.

By the time they had bought everything on her mama's list, when added to the bags containing Elliott's purchases, the trunk compartment was filled to overflowing. Elliott struggled with some creative rearranging, tucked a few items under the seat, then pressed down on her mama's cotton yarn with considerable force, still barely managing to close the trunk.

He shook his head as he started the engine. "If you can't tell, I've never shopped with women before, and I don't think I will again. This also reminds me, I want to pay for my share of the groceries."

"Hush, Elliott. You are doing work worth more than the cost of feeding you by helping John. I don't know what we would do without you. Right, Louise?"

This time, Louise got the window seat, and her mother sat in the middle. She missed sitting beside Elliott, and her mother's words interrupted her thoughts contemplating how she could ask if perhaps the next time their family needed goods, if she could take the list and go alone with Elliott.

She turned away from the window, nodding as she spoke. "Yes. Especially on the stairs. I don't think Papa would accept our help, but he doesn't question or complain when you make sure he goes slowly and doesn't fall."

"I'm glad to be of help."

"I hope everyone has worked up an appetite shopping, because when we get home, there is a pot of stew simmering. I hope John has been able to put more wood in the stove like I asked him to. Shopping always makes me hungry. What about you, Elliott? Are you hungry?"

"I'll never turn down your good cooking, Mrs. Demchuck."

"Unfortunately, since we've been out all day, Louise and I haven't made a dessert. Can you believe this is the first time since you've been staying with us that we won't have dessert?"

"But Mama, there are still cookies left from yesterday."

"Yes, I suppose they will have to do."

"You ladies are spoiling me, but I am not going to complain."

Louise watched Elliott smile, and he made no further comments as he continued to drive. The lines on his face weren't so prominent as they had been a week ago, which meant that, despite the hard work, all the extra treats were doing what they were meant to do. She tried to imagine what he would look like by the time he left, with his thin frame more filled out than at present.

And that reminded Louise that the next seven weeks were going to go by much too fast.

Rather than allow herself to dwell on him leaving, she chose to enjoy the rest of the day. Today, she would participate in the conversation inside the car and not dwell on things she couldn't change.

Her mama gasped and pointed out the window. "Look! Another deer! Did anyone see it?"

≈

"Amen," Elliott said aloud with the rest of the congregation at the close of the service.

He stood at the same time as the rest of the people present but didn't file outside. Instead, he waited at the end of the pew for Louise to return from the organ.

In the past week, he'd never once had the opportunity to hear her play. Every evening, a delicious dinner along with a delectable dessert had been ready as soon as he and John arrived back to the house after the day's work was done. Immediately following dinner, he spent at least two hours with John at the desk, learning as much as he could about the specific duties of the section foreman as well as background information and history of the railroad. The knowledge gave him a greater understanding of what happened beyond John's thirty miles of track. As well, it showed him the magnitude of the details the district office had to oversee in order to ensure everything was in perfect order to keep the trains running every minute of every day.

While this was far from his choice of the ideal job, Elliott was grateful beyond thoughts or words to have it. A week ago he'd sent a letter to Ike to advise him of the delay in his planned arrival to the West Coast. He'd asked Ike to locate Edward's address and forward a second letter he'd enclosed. So far he had not heard from Edward, but considering what Ike had to do to forward his letter on its way, he knew he couldn't expect a reply yet. All he could do was hope that when his time working for the railroad was over, he still had the opportunity for employment in the logging industry, which wasn't his ideal choice, either. However, at this point in his life, like countless other men, he would take anything he was offered to provide an income, permanent or temporary.

A pause in the music brought Elliott's thoughts back to Louise and where he was, but she turned the page and played another hymn, filling time until most of the congregation dispersed.

Elliott smiled as he listened to the music. Louise played the organ beautifully, even more outstanding than her mother had promised. He also knew from standing beside her during the service last week that Louise sang as well as she played, despite her protests and denials.

While the music continued, a deep male voice sounded behind him.

"Greetings! Louise tells me you're new on the section gang. I'm Nicholas Sabinski, but everyone calls me Nick. I couldn't help but hear you sing. My daughter Minnie tells me that where you come from you were part of a barbershop quartet. I've always wanted to do something like that, and I was wondering if you would consider helping us start such a group here in Pineridge."

Elliott recognized him as the man in the congregation who sang the bold bass harmony, and he recognized the name as the man who owned the town's general store, if he could call this burg of eight buildings a town.

He stiffened and tucked his hands into his pockets. "I'd love to, Nick, but I'm only going to be here for seven more weeks, until John is out of the cast. And then I'll be on my way to British Columbia. Otherwise, I'd be glad to."

"Would you consider helping us get such a group started until you leave? I've spoken to a few of the men here, and they are interested in doing both hymns for the Sunday service, as well as other numbers just for fun. And as far as a quartet, there are actually five of us if we count you. We'd like to meet every second or third Saturday afternoon."

Elliott couldn't help his smile. What Nick was explaining was exactly what his group back home was like. They had seven permanent members, and a few other men who dropped in and out as time and energy permitted. He glanced over at Louise, who now was slipping her hymnal and some loose music into the bench. He had been looking forward to spending as much of his remaining time as possible with her, especially since so far the only time he'd spent with her was when they sat together at church. While he'd enjoyed their shopping trip yesterday, they'd been far from alone.

Since Nick indicated that only a few hours of his time would be needed, and not every week, the suggestion gained more appeal. "That does sound like it could be fun. Do you have a place to meet? I don't have transportation."

"Pastor Galbraith says we can use this church building, since it's central and has the organ."

"That's great."

As Louise joined them, Nick nodded a greeting but kept speaking to Elliott. "You don't happen to play the organ or piano, do you?"

"I'm afraid I don't."

Nick frowned and crossed his arms. "That's one thing that has been keeping us from doing this. I'm the only one who can read music, and none of us can play an instrument."

Elliott nodded. "I can also read music, but I can't play an instrument, either."

Louise's eyebrows scrunched in the middle, something Elliott so far hadn't seen. He figured she looked absolutely adorable. "What are you planning that you need an organist? Is there something I can do for you, Mr. Sabinski?"

Nick turned to Elliott. "Mildred Johnstone and Louise are the only ones in our congregation who can play the organ or piano." His smile softened, and he turned to Louise. "I couldn't help but be impressed with Elliott's fine voice in church. I'm trying to convince this young man to help us start a men's singing group. We've got use of the organ, but I think a group singing in harmony would require at least someone who can read music enough to show us the notes we're supposed to be singing." Nick returned his gaze to Elliott. "I don't suppose you would happen to have any music with you? Although I would think we would start on the hymns, which of course we have access to. As if we could read anything besides the words." He turned to grin at Elliott.

"Sorry, but I didn't bring anything like that with me." He didn't want to tell Mr. Sabinski the full extent of what he hadn't arrived with into their community.

Louise turned her head and looked at the organ as she spoke. "I could probably help you. There are quite a few songs for groups in the pile of music in the bench. I don't know why, because I don't think our church has ever had a choir. But I suppose we could make some changes so they could be for men only."

Nick smiled, then reached to shake Elliott's hand. "Great. Can we start next Saturday at two o'clock?"

Elliott nodded. It wasn't like he had anything else to do or anywhere else to go. Also, now that Louise had agreed to help, this was a good way to spend time with her in a pleasant environment away from her parents' house, even if they wouldn't be alone. "I think that's a good time. Louise?"

At her answering smile, something funny happened in his stomach, making him wonder if he was hungry.

"Yes, that sounds good. I'll see you then, Mr. Sabinski. I only ask for one thing."

"Anything. Name it."

"Please do not think of singing 'I've Been Working on the Railroad.' "

eleven

Louise sat on a comfortably flat rock as she carefully selected the largest and plumpest strawberries and dropped them into her pail. As she picked, she kept Elliott in view out of the corner of her eye.

Elliott had also chosen to sit while he picked. Never in her life had Louise ever seen her papa pick berries with her mama, but when Mama suggested Elliott join her, he had accompanied her without hesitation.

The first time she'd seen Elliott he had been eating strawberries from this same patch. She didn't know what kind of berries grew near Katona Falls, but these strawberries were among the best early berries she'd ever seen. Apparently, Elliott felt the same, because for every one strawberry that made it into Elliott's pail, at least two went into his mouth.

She studied him in silence. She couldn't help but compare the unkempt and bedraggled man of barely over a week ago to the man before her now. Knowing now what she didn't know then, she could only guess at how hungry he must have been. So far he had successfully avoided saying much about his experiences on the freight trains, but he'd told her much of his life back in Katona Falls.

While she'd come to know him fairly quickly in some ways, in other ways she didn't know him at all. She had hoped if they could ever spend time together without her parents or a crowd around him, they could talk more freely about things that really mattered. She wanted to know more than his history. She knew he was a man of faith, but she also wanted to know his hopes and his dreams, even if at this point his dreams were all he had left.

Louise settled the strawberries in her pail, which was now half full. She couldn't see how much Elliott had in his pail, but she suspected it wasn't much.

"This works better if you eat only one for every other one put in the pail."

In one quick movement, he dumped the small handful of berries from the pail into his hand, popped the whole handful into his mouth, then held the pail upside down and shook it. "Then I think I'll have to start over," he said, doing rather poorly at talking around the berries in his mouth.

Even stuffed with berries, his cheeks were thin but better than they were a week ago. Unfortunately, having cakes and desserts every day was also doing the same for her as it did for him, but she could ill afford to gain much weight. Today, they were going to make a strawberry and rhubarb pie. If she could get enough strawberries.

He turned and began to pick again, and this time, since his mouth was still overstuffed, the entire handful of berries made it into his pail.

"I didn't want to ask you this in front of Papa at lunchtime, but how did your first solo track inspection go this morning?"

"It went fine."

Louise continued to pick, not looking up as she spoke. "I mean really. It's okay. Papa isn't here to listen to what you say. How are you managing with the section gang? I know it's hard work. Even when jobs are hard to find, the men tend to come and go."

"It's hard work, to be sure, but I think I'm getting more used to it. And very honestly, the track inspection went well this morning. I don't think I'll have any problems." He paused for a few seconds, allowing Louise to hear the plunking of the berries as they bounced in the bottom of the metal pail. "So far the hardest part is moving the speedster by myself. That thing is heavy."

"I wouldn't think that being on the section gang was like

any job you'd ever thought of doing. You said before that you had attended university until you had to quit. What course were you taking? What did you really intend on doing?"

Suddenly, Louise clamped her mouth shut. She couldn't believe the words had actually slipped out of her mouth. She'd wondered and thought about him so much that she hadn't been aware she'd asked out loud until it was too late.

Unable to face him as she spoke, she turned all her concentration to picking the berries in front of her. "Please forgive me for asking such personal questions. It's none of my business. I have such bad timing. I can only guess at how hard this whole thing is for you." Louise paused for a few seconds and cleared her throat. "How much do you have in your pail? I think we must have enough to make a pie by now."

"It's okay, Louise. I know you're curious. In your position, I'd be curious too."

She could feel the heat in her cheeks, but she raised her head and met his gaze to listen to his words.

"My hope was to become a mathematician and, with that, be a university professor. The way things have gone over the last few years, that's not going to happen now. I'm already twenty-five years old, and I don't see any chance of going back to university in the foreseeable future. Even if I could scrape together the tuition and books, I'd still need living expenses. All I can do is trust in God's will for me and follow the path I believe He's set out. I can't see where that is yet, but I have to trust that one day, I will."

"Is that why you accepted Papa's job offer? Working on the section gang can't compare to being a university professor."

One corner of his mouth crooked up. "Neither is working in a logging camp. For now, I have to go where I can earn an income. I believe in miracles, but I also believe that not all miracles come in the form of handouts. Sometimes, when God provides, what He provides is opportunity, and sometimes it involves work."

"Yes, that is true."

"Tell me about yourself, Louise. You're what, nineteen? What do you want to do with your life?"

"Actually, I'm almost twenty. Since I like to cook, and since it's been so satisfying for me to help people by feeding them, in the fall I'm going to go to college to become a dietician. Papa thinks that's a good idea, as opposed to what my friends would rather do. They want to move into the city and just take any type of job so they can meet someone and get married. Papa says I shouldn't be in a rush to get married; there's plenty of time for that."

"Your papa is right."

"I only want to get married when God places the right person in my path. When that happens, I figure I should know it. Do you think that happens?"

His voice took on a husky edge, making Louise wonder if he'd swallowed something strange with the berries. "Yes, I do. It happened that way with my brother. I'm praying that one day that will happen to me, too."

"Louise! Elliott!" her mama's voice echoed from the distance.

Louise raised one hand to her lips. "It's Mama! She's waiting for these berries! How much do you have in your pail?"

Elliott's cheeks darkened. "Not much, I'm embarrassed to admit. What about you?"

"Coming, Mama!" she called out. Louise dumped a portion of her berries into Elliott's pail and lowered her voice, although she didn't know why. Her mother obviously couldn't hear her from where she was. "Come on. We'd better hurry. I think there's enough to make a pie."

He stared down into the pail. "Louise? What are you doing? I doubt your mama will care that I hardly picked any berries."

For a brief second, she considered taking the berries back. "I don't know. We had better go."

She hurried down the path with Elliott following close

behind, until they arrived back at the house and placed both pails on the table.

Her mama stared down into the pails. She remained silent, her brows knotted, and she jiggled both pails slightly.

Behind her, Elliott cleared his throat. "I'm sorry, Mrs. Demchuck. The berries were so good I'm afraid I ate more than I brought back. If this isn't enough, I'll go back and pick more. And this time, I promise not to eat them."

"I suppose this will be enough to make one pie. If you've eaten so much, I do hope that you will be able to eat your dinner. Today I cooked that ham that we bought yesterday. It's such a treat to get a ham that's so tender and juicy; we don't get them often. And as a special treat, I'm making a salad with head lettuce and crisp celery!"

Louise saw Elliott blink. His eyebrows raised, but he didn't comment.

She stepped closer. "Head lettuce and celery are not grown by our local farmers. The only time we can enjoy a nice fresh salad is after a trip to Beauséjour or Winnipeg."

"You mean you can only make a salad once every two weeks, after driving two or more hours to go shopping?"

"Yes. Living here in the country is nothing like living in the city."

Elliott turned back to her mother and covered his stomach with his hand. "I can assure you, Mrs. Demchuck, none will be wasted. Have I told you recently how much you are spoiling me?"

Her mother grinned back. "I think you said something to that effect at lunchtime. Now if you'll excuse us, Louise and I must get busy or no one will be eating."

The soothing strains of the classical music coming from the radio were interrupted by the low murmur of voices when Elliott joined her papa on the couch.

"I was beginning to wonder if you'd been eaten by a bear."

"I'm sorry, Mama. We started talking and I forgot all about

picking." She covered her mouth with her hands but couldn't cover up her giggle. "But you should have seen him. He was really funny eating the strawberries. When he caught me looking, he put them into the pail, but when he thought I wasn't looking, everything he picked, he ate."

"I don't know why you're laughing. You used to do that when you were a little girl."

"I suppose I did. I guess I thought I was getting away with it. It must be true that mothers have eyes in the back of their heads."

"Not really. If you don't get busy, dinner won't be ready for a very long time. And I don't need eyes in the back of my head to know that."

≈

Elliott stood to the side of the jigger to help John support himself while Frank stayed on the jigger's deck to help John balance. John leaned on the crutches, barely staying upright as he watched Elliott and Frank and Henry hoist the heavy jigger off the track and onto the ties. Together they pushed the unit into the toolhouse for the night and said their good-byes.

Elliott joined John, and they slowly made their way over the tracks and to the house, where John nearly collapsed by the time they made it to the couch.

John swiped his sleeve over his forehead and his head fell to the back of the couch. "I hardly did anything today, but I'm exhausted. I don't want to think of what the next seven weeks will be like."

Without being asked, Mrs. Demchuck appeared with a glass of water, which John drank gratefully, then closed his eyes to rest.

Elliott couldn't help but feel sorry for John. While just as he said, John didn't do much, Elliott could see the difficulty involved in any movement with the cast. The weight of it alone was daunting.

Last week, John had remained on the jigger while he and

the section men went about their duties. Today, at John's insistence, they had helped him down off the jigger when they arrived at the particular tie that needed replacing. They could see John was getting bored with staying in one spot for so long and, even though he wouldn't admit it, he was starting to become irritable.

Today they were working on replacing ties, which meant John had been off and back on the jigger numerous times, and the strain showed. Helping him get on and off the jigger wasn't doing wonders for Frank or Henry, either.

Then, John had been so tired that they had packed up earlier than usual, just to take him home.

Elliott hadn't wanted to be at the house at this particular time. Today, the freight train was stopping to unload a shipment for Nick. And that meant Elliott would be watching from an entirely different perspective.

Today, he would be watching the homeless men on the 6:15 freight train not as one of them but as an employee of the railroad.

Technically it was the job of the brakeman to clear the hobos from the freight cars, but when John was in the area, he was also required to as well.

Elliott knew the hard way that even if the men were removed from the train in a place such as this, they had nowhere to go. He also knew that because it was his duty, John went through the motions to remove the homeless men from the trains, as did the brakeman, but everyone knew they would get back on. Neither John nor the brakeman did anything to stop them. There was nothing they could do.

This time, since the train was stopping long enough for a shipment to be dropped off, that meant the men riding the boxcars would be able to wander around until the train departed. Most of them would hide, but some of them were bound to go searching for food.

According to Louise, some of them would come knocking

on the door, begging for food. For anyone who asked, none would be turned away.

Just he had not been turned away.

The women remained in the kitchen preparing dinner and doing laundry, and beside him on the couch, John nodded off to sleep. A long whistle sounded in the distance, indicating the pending arrival of the freight train, followed by a low rumble, increasing in volume. The house only shook slightly this time because the train actually stopped.

When all was quiet, Elliott closed his eyes. He didn't expect to hear much, but he knew what was happening. He had no intention of going outside to clear the train of hobos. Instead, he kept his eyes closed, bowed his head, and prayed for the men, whoever they were, on that train and all the trains across the continent. He prayed for their safety, for opportunity, and for them to find other good-hearted people like the Demchucks as they continued on their way.

His mind went blank when he heard a knock on the back door. Until today, he'd been working or waiting on a siding with the rest of the section gang when the freight trains passed. Today was the first time he was at the house when a freight train stopped.

The knock meant someone had come to beg for food—a man just like him who had come off the freight trains—a man so hungry he had been reduced to begging.

Today it was Louise who answered the door. He listened to the drone of their conversation, and even though he couldn't hear the words, he knew that Louise was gladly giving the man food, sharing a brief message that Jesus loved him enough to die for him, and sending him outside with a plate of food.

He still didn't know why he had been the only homeless man to be invited inside, nor did he understand why he had been chosen to be so blessed by them. Not only did they provide food and lodging and a job, but their actions extended past mere ministry. They welcomed him into their home and even adjusted their own lifestyle to suit him. He could tell they were going to bed earlier than usual in order to give him some privacy as he fell into an exhausted sleep every night on their couch. He doubted they regularly slept nine hours every night, but at this point, he needed to take advantage of their kindness in order to develop his endurance—both to the hard work and to the noise of the trains as they passed, to his dismay, every few hours, all night, every night.

He would never be able to pay them back, but at the same time, he knew they didn't want him to.

Elliott buried his face in his hands, trying to figure out what God was trying to teach him. If he ever in his life was to be able to provide a ministry to others, he wanted to do it like the Demchucks. They didn't set themselves apart. Instead, they followed the example of Jesus and treated the people they helped as equals, not as second-class citizens as he'd so often seen people do.

Part of him wanted to go outside and talk to the men who came off the freight train, even though he had nothing to give, but he couldn't force himself to get off the couch. In addition to accepting their kindness and their food, he'd accepted money from these warmhearted people because it would still be almost two weeks before he received his first paycheck. For now, his wounds were still too raw. However, Elliott made up his mind that as soon as he was able to do so, he would follow the Demchucks' example and help those less fortunate than himself.

"Papa! Elliott! Come for dinner!"

Elliott stood in front of John, waiting. When John became aware of his surroundings and was alert enough to stand, Elliott extended one hand to help pull him up off the couch. At the same time, the train pulled away from the station.

Today, he wanted to be the one to lead in a prayer of thanks. He had a lot to be thankful for.

twelve

Elliott laid the tongs on the ground, then dropped to his knees to help Henry push the new tie into position. When it looked right, Elliott stood back to wipe the sweat from his brow while Frank kicked the tamping bar to set the ballast around the new tie.

"Kick it over a little to the left," John called from his seat atop the jigger, which was pulled off onto the siding.

When it looked good, Elliott measured its distance from the other ties on each side to make sure it was centered and level. "It's good," he called out.

Together, Elliott and Henry slid in the tie plates to support the rails, and John pulled the new spikes out of the box. Frank picked up the spike maul and drove the first spike through the tie plate. He was about to pound in the second one when Elliott raised his palm to stop him. "Wait. Do you hear that?" His heart pounded in his chest to think that a train was coming and they had not completely replaced the tie. He squinted and stared down the parallel lengths of track. "Something's coming, but the train isn't due for half an hour. Besides, that's too small." He also didn't feel the ground trembling, which was always a warning that a train was approaching.

John, Frank, and Henry groaned in unison.

"Not today!" John called out to the sky.

Elliott let his mouth hang open at the sight of a car coming. . .down the tracks.

"But. . . ," he muttered, then snapped his mouth shut. Suddenly he understood.

If he thought he was sweating before, he was definitely sweating now.

This was it. His first inspection by the road master.

Frank and Henry helped John down from the jigger while Elliott watched a black sedan approach on the tracks. Instead of rubber tires, the car rode on miniature train wheels which set it perfectly and efficiently on the track. The car slowed as it neared the switch, then stopped. A man got out, threw the handle on the railway switch, drove the car onto the siding, got out of the car once again, flipped the switch back, then continued on toward them.

John's voice dropped to a mumble. "His name is Heinrich Getz."

Elliott lowered his voice so he could speak to John without Frank and Henry hearing. "Your supervisor?"

"Yes and no. He's not my direct supervisor, but my supervisor gets his report. Heinrich's comments and opinions of my section affect my supervisor's appraisal of the job performance of my crew, and that affects me."

The car came to a stop a few feet away from the jigger. A tall and rather handsome man a few years older than Elliott exited the car carrying a clipboard. Elliott stepped forward to meet him and stretched out his hand.

"I'm Elliott Endicott, John's new lead hand. Pleased to meet you."

Heinrich's brows knotted as he glanced at John leaning on the crutches. He quickly met Elliott's eye contact and returned the handshake. "Heinrich Getz, road master. Yes, I've heard that John hired a new lead hand." He turned to John. "It looks like you've had a bit of an accident."

"Yes. Nothing too serious."

Heinrich smiled. "Looks serious to me, but it's nice to see it's not keeping you from working." He took a pen out of his pocket, checked the time, and made a few notes on the top page of the clipboard, glanced down at John's cast, then back to the clipboard. "You know the routine, John. Or should I go through this with your lead hand?"

"You can go through it with me. Elliott, you can finish up, and when the train passes, go to the next one without me."

Elliott nodded. As lead hand, he should have gone to over- see Frank and Henry, but his feet remained fixed. John started to make his way to the car Heinrich had come in, which meant crossing the siding tracks to get into the passenger side of Heinrich's car. So far, every time John crossed the tracks Elliott had assisted him, first making his precarious way over the rocks which surrounded the tracks, then finding a firm footing for the crutches on the tarred wooden ties. Also, the process of getting the cast over the height of the metal rails on crutches required considerable orchestration.

To Elliott's surprise, Heinrich smiled and carefully helped John through the rocks, then waited for John to position the crutches on the best spot on a tie. He then slipped one arm around John's waist and allowed John to lean on him as he lifted the cast over the rails, just as Elliott had done for the past week and a half.

He swallowed hard, then turned to Frank and Henry. In John's absence, this would be his first time officially super- vising John's section men. He hoped and prayed he was up to the task.

Elliott watched as Frank pounded in the last spike. After checking the tie when all the work was complete and finding everything satisfactory, they shoveled the displaced rocks back into place, packed up the tools, and loaded them onto the jigger.

Out of the corner of his eye, every now and then Elliott stole a glance at Heinrich's car, still parked beside the jigger. Both doors remained open as John and Heinrich discussed what was written on the papers attached to Heinrich's clipboard.

The ground started to tremble. Elliott pulled on the chain attached to his belt loop to draw out the pocket watch John had loaned him. "Right on time," he mumbled.

He climbed aboard the jigger, along with Frank and Henry,

and waited for the train to pass. When it did, the engine of Heinrich's car roared to life. Elliott pushed down on the jigger's handle, and slowly, they made their way to the switch. Once there, Elliott jumped off the jigger and set the switch to allow the jigger to go from the siding to the main track. Once it passed, he reset the switch and they backed up the jigger to sit behind the intersection of track next to the switch. After setting it again, they signaled, and the road master's car passed them and continued on, heading down the track to the station at Pineridge. Elliott watched it disappear into the distance, reset the switch for the last time for the next train to pass straight through, then clambered back aboard the jigger.

"Okay, let's get going," Elliott muttered. "And after the next one's done, we'll call it a day."

The next tie they replaced went as smoothly as the previous one, boosting Elliott's confidence in his new leadership capabilities. This time, he sat on the bench while Frank and Henry pumped the jigger's handle as they made it back to the Pineridge station in plenty of time before the evening freight train.

The road master's car remained parked on the siding at the station, even after they removed the jigger from the track and pushed it into the toolhouse.

Elliott bade good night to the other men, then walked to the Demchucks' house.

When he opened the back door, he expected to see both Mrs. Demchuck and Louise busy preparing dinner, but only Mrs. Demchuck was in the kitchen.

He kicked off his boots and tucked them into the corner of the boot tray, then slipped off the denim overalls and hung them on the hook on the back of the door. After he smoothed some of the wrinkles out of his trousers, Mrs. Demchuck walked up to him and helped him brush the wrinkles out of the sleeves of his shirt.

"You're early, which is good. We've invited Heinrich to

stay for dinner, and we have to eat early so he can get to Winnipeg before nightfall, as he's booked into a hotel there for the night."

At the mention that the road master would be staying, Elliott glanced at the kitchen table. Instead of being set for dinner, it was spread with the bowls and utensils Mrs. Demchuck had been using to prepare their meal.

"I know what you're thinking. We'll be eating in the dining room today."

"I guess Heinrich is a special guest."

"Yes, he is. As you have no doubt seen, we don't get many visitors. We like to treat all our guests as special, but I must admit that we give Heinrich better treatment than most. Now you go into the living room, and I'll call everyone when dinner is ready."

Since Louise was absent from the kitchen, Elliott wondered if she had made an unexpected errand to their favorite local farmer again to purchase the ingredients for a treat for the road master.

As he thought about it, he walked into the living room to wait for her return. His feet skidded to a halt when he saw Louise sitting in the center of the couch with John on one side and Heinrich on the other. She was laughing at something someone had said, but when she saw him, her laughter faded.

"Glad to see you here before the freight train," John said. "Bring yourself the chair from the desk and please join us."

Elliott preferred to remain standing, but he wouldn't contradict his host in front of their distinguished guest.

Conversation had not yet resumed when Mrs. Demchuck called them for dinner.

John led everyone in prayer over the food, and Mrs. Demchuck and Louise served creamed chicken. Elliott knew they had no cream in the outdoor cellar, so Louise had made that special trip to visit the local farmer, as he suspected.

Elliott expected conversation would have centered around

work-related projects, but instead, Heinrich spent most of his time talking to Louise. At first, Elliott found it strange that Heinrich knew her so well, but then he remembered John telling him that the road master paid every section foreman a monthly visit.

Since Elliott was new and since his method of arrival had been somewhat less than ideal, Elliott chose to add little to the conversation. As the meal continued, Heinrich talked more and more, entertaining everyone with his stories. Elliott found himself laughing with the others at the interesting twists, although it was more than obvious parts of the stories had been embellished for entertainment value.

At the end of the meal, instead of retiring to the living room, John saw Heinrich out the door and to the car on the siding. With Mrs. Demchuck and Louise in the kitchen cleaning up, Elliott made his way into the living room. He sat on the couch to listen to the radio, but he didn't do much listening. Instead, as he sat alone, he did some thinking.

If he looked out the window from his place on the couch, he could see John and Heinrich talking.

Heinrich appeared to be a good man and a likable fellow. For his age, which appeared to be in his early to mid thirties, he carried a job with much responsibility. From the way John spoke of him, he appeared to do it well, and Heinrich had earned the respect of all the section gangs under his jurisdiction. Frank and Henry liked him, John liked him, and even Mrs. Demchuck liked him. Elliott thought that he would have liked Heinrich a little more if Louise didn't appear to also like him.

Elliott watched as John and Heinrich walked to the toolhouse, where they disappeared inside. A few minutes later, they exited the small building, shook hands, and Heinrich walked to his car on the tracks. The engine roared to life and started to pull away. Rather than watch John struggle over the tracks with the crutches, Elliott sprang to his feet and jogged to John, barely beating him to the set of tracks.

In the distance, the road master's car stopped. Heinrich exited the car, set the switch, drove off the siding onto the main track, exited the car to close the switch, and the car began its journey down the tracks.

Elliott stood beside John as they watched him disappear in the distance.

"Will he make it to Winnipeg before dark?"

John nodded. "Yes. He can't go very fast, but you must admit, it's a very direct route."

Elliott didn't look at John as he spoke. "It appears he didn't know about your injury."

"No, I didn't tell him, nor is there really a way to do so, except on the morning scheduling call. My job is only to supervise and guarantee the quality of the maintenance and repairs on my section, but I tend to do extra and often pitch in and do some of the heavy work when necessary. Within reason, of course."

"He didn't say much to me. Is that normal?"

"I think he was surprised to see you join us at dinner. Anna doesn't invite the section men in for dinner, not even the lead hand, when Heinrich comes for his monthly inspection. I have to warn you, though, he did question where you'd come from, because he's never seen you before. Usually the lead hand position is awarded to someone who has been on their particular section gang for awhile, or at least it's someone who has had experience with another section gang."

Elliott crossed his arms, then turned to John. The road master's car had long since disappeared from sight, yet they still stood beside the track. "My being here won't cause a problem, will it?"

"Shouldn't."

John continued to stare down the empty track, his brows knotted.

After a few minutes of silence, Elliott turned toward the

house. Even though John would never admit it, Elliott could tell the events of the day were taking their toll on him. "Let's get back to the house. I think it might start to rain soon."

Neither spoke as Elliott assisted John over the tracks. Louise met them at the door, shuffling her feet while she waited for Elliott to help John up the few steps to the house.

"Papa, I was at McSorbins' farm today. They have some chicks ready for me. Can I pick them up tomorrow?"

Elliott blinked. "Chicks?"

John nodded and smiled as he slowly thumped his way across the room on the crutches. Elliott helped John lower himself onto the couch, and then John resumed speaking.

"Every year we get some chicks for Louise from one of the local farms."

Louise smiled at her father. "Can Elliott drive me in the car to go get them when you come back from work tomorrow?"

John turned to Elliott. "Don't ask me. Ask Elliott."

She turned to him and smiled so brightly Elliott had to remind himself to breathe. "Elliott?"

He cleared his throat. "I suppose I can drive you. Where are you going to put them?"

"Mama and I found the crate from last year in the basement. Can you bring it up for me?"

"Crate? You keep chickens in a crate?"

"Of course I don't keep them in a crate. They only stay in it until they're big enough to go outside."

Elliott shook his head. He wasn't sure he wanted to ask the next question, but he had to. "Do you mean to say that you bring animals into the house?"

"They're very young and have to be kept warm. It still gets too cold at night, so we keep them beside the cookstove until they are strong enough. Every year we lose a few, but Mr. McSorbin gives them to me for a lower cost if I buy them when they are this size. He needs the room for his own chicks that his family will keep and sell themselves when they get big enough. They also give me a better discount if I bring my own box to take them home in."

Before he could ask any more questions, Louise had already left the room. He followed her into the kitchen, then down to the farthest corner of the basement to a pile of wood, a reel of wire mesh, a stack of stakes and poles, and an orange crate.

He stood behind her as she bent down, brushed some dust off the orange crate, picked it up, stood, and handed it to him.

"So how was it?" she asked.

"Pardon me?"

"The inspection. Did Heinrich say anything?"

"No, he didn't. Should he have?"

"Not really, but I heard some of what he was asking Papa while they were at the desk. That was before I had to leave to get the cream from the McSorbins. He asked Papa who you were and where you came from and who was doing the track inspections."

Elliott's dinner went to war with his stomach. "Did I miss something or do something wrong?"

"It didn't sound like it. I heard Papa tell him that you had done the track inspection a few times when he wasn't able to. If he hasn't said anything to you, then everything must be fine."

"I know that Heinrich came to do an inspection, but does he usually stay for dinner?"

Louise tilted her head, and one eye narrowed. "Actually, no, he usually comes earlier, in the mornings; and Mama always asks him to stay for lunch, which he does. Now that you mention it, it is a little odd that he came so late and stayed for dinner."

Elliott also thought it was strange that for a supposed business visit, very little of it was actually business. Most of his time was spent talking to Louise.

"Does he always spend so much time visiting with you when he's here to talk to your father?"

She blinked twice and crossed her arms over her chest. "I don't know. He's always been friendly to me. Just today he—"

John's voice drifted from upstairs. "Louise! Come quickly! That cooking program is on the radio! They're talking about that chicken dish you tried before!"

"Oh! I have to go!" Louise turned and ran to the stairs.

Elliott extended the orange crate slightly forward. "Wait! What do you want me to do with this?"

She turned her head and spoke over her shoulder as she ascended the stairs. "Put it outside by the back door. For tomorrow."

With her words, she reached the top of the stairs and disappeared into the kitchen.

Elliott stared at the orange crate in his hands. It was nothing that Louise couldn't have carried herself, and he wondered why she had brought him downstairs.

He shrugged his shoulders, walked upstairs and outside, and laid the crate on the ground, as requested. Before he went back in the house, he stared down into it and smiled, imagining three or four cute little baby chicks inside.

thirteen

Louise slipped the cheesecloth over the bushel of grain she'd purchased for feed and carefully tucked in the corners. She stood back to admire her creativeness, then pushed the trunk of the car closed. "That should be it. I don't think any will spill on the way home." She turned to Elliott, who had the orange crate containing the chicks in his hands. "We should go quickly. They won't stay very warm like that."

He stared down into the wooden crate. "How many are in here?"

Louise stood aside and opened the car door. "Two dozen. They're bigger than the ones I had last year. Maybe I won't lose any of these."

Elliott slid the crate into the center of the seat. "Twenty-four chickens. . . ," he muttered under his breath as he stepped aside to allow her to get in. When she was sitting comfortably, he closed the door and walked around the car, giving her enough time to pick up one of the darling little chicks before the driver's door opened and he slid in behind the steering wheel.

Nestled into her hand, the little chick curled into a ball and fell asleep. She gently ran her finger over the yellow fuzz that would soon be turning to feathers, then held it out to give Elliott the chance to pet the chick, too, which he did.

"Isn't she cute?"

"She certainly is. What are you going to do with all those chickens? Would you really use two dozen eggs a day?"

Louise shook her head. "They wouldn't start laying until late fall, but by then, most of them will be eaten."

At her words, he jerked his hand back and his face paled.

"Why are you looking at me like that? You enjoyed the creamed chicken Mama made for dinner yesterday."

"Yes, but I didn't have to look it in the eye before I ate it."

"It's not a dog, and it's not a pet. It's a chicken."

He started the car, not looking at her as he spoke. "Still. . ." His voice trailed off.

Louise couldn't hold back her smile. "You really are a city boy, aren't you?"

He turned and grinned at her, and Louise's foolish heart fluttered. "Yes, it appears I am."

She set all her attention on the chicks in the crate between them. "We must seem so primitive to you. I know when we visit my aunt in Winnipeg and stay overnight, it feels like a trip to a palace. I think the thing I like the best is my aunt's icebox." She felt the heat rise to her cheeks. She wasn't going to say out loud that the real best part was not having to go outside to use the outhouse.

"I know. At home in Katona Falls, the iceman came right to my door twice a week. When I was growing up, all the children in the neighborhood used to love it when he gave us chips of ice to suck on."

Louise smiled, imagining him as a young child. "That sounds like fun. Of course you know we've never had an icebox, just the outdoor cellar. When I was a child, it used to be fun for my sister and me to pack snow in the outdoor cellar, but the older I got, the less fun it became, especially after she moved away. I guess that's probably why I think the icebox is the best part about living in the city. What do you like best about living in the city?"

Elliott grinned. "Hot water." He paused to glance at her, then turned his attention back to the road. "A few years ago, when business was still good, Ike installed a tank, kind of like a large boiler that keeps the water warm all the time so we don't have to keep filling up the kettle on the woodstove at the barbershop, especially in the summer. Since I lived in the suite upstairs, we ran a pipe upstairs. My friends loved to come over just to get hot water from the tap."

Louise turned her head and stared out the window, no longer interested in the chicks. Not that she was dissatisfied with her life in Pineridge; she enjoyed the simple lifestyle here, but she didn't want to appear uncivilized in his eyes. Not only did Elliott have running water, he had hot running water. Even her aunt didn't have hot running water, although Louise heard that the newer homes in the city did.

"I know what you're thinking, Louise. I don't mind having to pump the water and then wait for it to be heated. Aside from not having a few newer conveniences, your parents have a lovely home. Most of all, they're wonderful people. They've been so kind and gracious to open their home to me, a stranger."

Suddenly, Louise felt ashamed of her jealous thoughts. While it was true her home had none of the luxuries Elliott's home had, in reality Elliott no longer had a home. He owned nothing but one set of clothes. Everything else he had was borrowed from her father or purchased with money he'd borrowed. Worst of all, he'd had to rely on the charity of other people, for now her family, even to eat. His life had come to the point that if it weren't for her family, he wouldn't be eating now.

In the end, it was not material goods or the luxuries of modern conveniences that mattered. Elliott had lost everything he'd ever held dear and was left to rely on God's grace and the charity of strangers for his very survival. Because of that, Louise could see that underneath all the things that could hide a person's true self, Elliott Endicott was a man of faith and fine character.

Louise cleared her throat. "I suppose I would be safe to assume that you've never raised chickens before."

"I've never had the opportunity to raise any kind of animal before."

"Then you're in luck. Every spring Papa gets a pig. We fatten it up all summer and then slaughter it in the fall after we have enough snow in the outdoor cellar and it gets cold enough to keep the meat frozen until it's used up. Maybe this year, you can get the pig for Papa and take care of it for him until he gets the cast off."

"I think I'll pass. I'd probably name it and teach it tricks like a dog. I couldn't bear to know that it would soon be coming to an untimely end. Everything I eat I've bought from the store, ready to cook without having to do anything else first or know any of the gory details, and I like it that way."

As Elliott stopped the car, Louise realized they had arrived at home. She hadn't been aware of most of the journey. Before she figured out what he was doing, Elliott had slipped out of the car, opened her door, and he stood to the side to allow her to get out. When she stood beside him, he leaned inside, reaching for the crate of chicks. "None of them are going to jump out on me, are they?"

"They're not frogs. Baby chicks do hop a little bit, but they certainly don't jump that high at this age."

"I don't know about that. All I know is that they're bouncing now."

As he backed out of the car while steadying the orange crate in front of him, he bumped into her from behind. He straightened quickly, and the sudden movement caused the chicks to cheep loudly. Automatically, Louise reached to steady the crate, and as she did so, her hand brushed his. Their gazes met, and he slowly brushed the back of her hand with his thumb.

Suddenly, Louise's heart started to pound out of control. "City boy," she muttered.

His hand covered hers completely. "Apparently," he mumbled, his voice unusually low in pitch.

Louise's throat clogged, and she couldn't respond with him touching her. She didn't know what happened, but something just had.

Without speaking, she yanked her hand away and ran into

the house, leaving Elliott to carry the chicks by himself.

&

"May I see some identification, please?"

Elliott stiffened. "I'm sorry, I don't have anything. My wallet has been stolen, and I haven't received my replacement driver's license or anything yet."

The bank teller paused, read the front of the check, then put it to the side. He picked up a form and his fountain pen. "Since you're opening an account, we can use a letter from another financial institution to verify your identity."

"I don't have anything like that. I'm new to the area, and I don't have anything set up yet. That's why I'm here. To open a new account."

The young man tapped the top of the pen to the counter. "Your address, then?"

Elliott shuffled his feet, wondering how many banks there could possibly be in Beauséjour. "I, uh, don't have an address. I'm staying with friends. In Pineridge. That's not too far from here. Would you like that one?"

Elliott gritted his teeth and forced himself to smile, hoping against good sense that the clerk wouldn't ask for their address because he didn't know it. No one used it, apparently not even the post office.

The clerk laid his pen on the counter, picked up Elliott's paycheck, read it again, turned it over to examine Elliott's signature, then folded his hands on the countertop. "Let me get this straight. You have no identification, no letters, no address, no other accounts in town, and you want to cash this check?"

"Yes, I do. It's a railway check. It's good."

"I'm sorry. I'm going to have to call for the manager. Please have a seat."

Elliott's stomach took a nosedive somewhere into the bottom of his shoes. It wasn't until he had the check in his hand that he'd realized he might have difficulty cashing it. He hadn't, however, expected this.

He left the teller's window and walked to the waiting area, where he stood beside Louise.

"What's taking so long? Why are we standing here?"

"They won't open an account and cash the check without seeing my identification, and I don't have any. Nor is there any local establishment they can contact to confirm I am who I say I am or that has my signature on file. Until I get something in writing, I'm stuck."

"What about asking your brother to send something? I hope your birth certificate wasn't in your wallet."

"No. That's the one thing that wasn't, but I'm hesitant to send the only identification I have left in the world through the mail, in case something happens to it. Besides, my birth certificate doesn't have my signature on it."

The teller returned. "Mr. Endicott? This way, please."

"I'm going with you," Louise whispered beside him.

He opened his mouth to tell her that wasn't necessary, but she was already ahead of him.

The teller ushered them into a private office. The manager leaned over his large wooden desk to shake Elliott's hand, waited for Louise to sit, and both men sat as well.

The manager folded his hands on the polished desktop. "I understand we have a bit of a problem."

It wasn't "a bit" of a problem. He had finally received his paycheck for his first week. Until he had the check in his hand, he hadn't known what his salary was to be. He'd heard the railroad paid well, and he found that to be true. After he cashed his paycheck for $16.89, he would have enough money to pay back what he owed the Demchucks from his last shopping trip. Then he could do more personal shopping, send some money to his brother, and have some for the offering at the church. He might even be able to buy himself a new Bible. He'd thought of buying himself a new wallet, but after all his expenses were taken care of, he doubted he would have anything to put in it. Therefore, that expenditure would wait for two weeks for his next shopping trip, when he would actually need a wallet. Still, he'd never made so much at the barbershop in one week, not even in two.

Elliott cleared his throat and faced the manager. "My wallet was stolen, so I have no identification. Also, I'm from out of town, so I have no local references."

"That's not true," Louise said, her voice causing both men to freeze. "I have an account here, and I can give him a reference. My name is Louise Demchuck." She started digging through her purse. "Here is my bankbook; I believe this is everything you'll need."

The bank manager smiled as he accepted it. "That will be fine, thank you." He stood, then leaned over to shake Elliott's hand once more. "I'll tell Randolph to set up that account for you. Good day, Mr. Endicott, Miss Demchuck."

As soon as the teller saw the door open, he appeared. The manager gave him Louise's bankbook and instructed him to set up the account.

Louise accompanied Elliott to the same grated window he'd been at previously and waited beside him while the teller filled out the information from Louise's file. Elliott stepped to the side when the teller directed her where to sign on the form, and he then continued to open the account.

He flinched when Louise touched his arm. "See? Everything is fine."

"Yes. Thank you." Elliott tried to smile, but inside he was numb.

It wasn't fine. A woman had to vouch for him. His ability to conduct financial transactions was in the hands of a woman who wasn't even legal age.

A few weeks ago, a man he had never met before had offered him a job, and he'd accepted it. He was now living in that man's house, sleeping on his couch, and driving his car.

That man's wife was feeding him.

Even their church and community had welcomed him

when he had nothing to offer.

Elliott felt like a flea living off the blood of a friendly dog. He was a parasite.

"You have to leave some money in the account to keep it open. How much shall I leave in, Mr. Endicott?"

"Whatever is the minimum."

The man counted out the money. "Thank you, Sir. I hope to see you again soon."

"Yes," Elliott mumbled. "You will. In exactly two weeks."

Louise was nearly skipping beside him as they walked down the main street. "Isn't it wonderful to have your own money, finally?"

He forced himself to smile. "Yes."

For longer than he cared to remember, Elliott had thought that all he needed to be happy was a job with a good income. Now he had it, but the hole in his soul seemed larger than ever. Eight weeks of a good salary didn't mean he was set for life, but for the near future, especially with no expenses beyond replacing the necessities and a few items for work, the money he earned would go a long way. In the end, though, it didn't make him as happy as he thought it would.

"The co-op at the corner of Derwent Street has the best prices for the overalls you'll need. And you can buy the boots at the co-op on Tarlton Street."

"Okay." His future was still hollow and uncertain. He'd never been shy for adventure, but Elliott didn't want adventure. He longed for the time he could spend his day at work, then spend his evenings at home in the good company of the woman who would be his wife and not have to worry about what the next day would or wouldn't bring.

"Mama gave me her grocery list, plus I have a couple of things to buy at the drugstore. What do you want to do first?"

"Makes no difference to me."

"I also want to buy Papa a good book. He's getting so bored and frustrated when all he can do is sit around all the time, and he's read everything in the house at least twice. Those two days it rained and he stayed home all day while you went to work, well, I've never seen Papa so restless. Can you help me pick out a good book for him?"

"Sure." He wondered what John liked to read, then thought he would have liked to buy John a book as a gift. Elliott felt his face tighten as he walked. He could well imagine John's reaction to his gift. Despite his best intentions, Elliott knew his host would not accept a gift from him graciously. John had made it more than clear that he didn't want Elliott to ever think of trying to pay him back. Even though he worked hard all day, the railroad paid well for that. When he accepted the job and all that went with it, Elliott had not foreseen how strange he'd feel about receiving free room and board. All his meals and needs were taken care of, merely for escorting John around the house and property and helping Mrs. Demchuck with tasks that John temporarily couldn't.

It unsettled Elliott to know he wasn't doing enough to reciprocate their kindness. Yet, when he managed to put the uneasiness aside, he felt happy at the Demchucks' home. The same bond existed between John and his wife that Elliott had seen between his own parents. As a young boy, he hadn't understood completely, but now, from an adult perspective, he did. He saw in the Demchucks' marriage the things he wanted for himself. As well as the love between husband and wife, they were best friends, something he didn't see very often. Just as his own parents were, John and Mrs. Demchuck were comfortable together, as well as apart.

He'd seen many of his friends fall in love so intensely that they couldn't bear to be separated, and then when they were together, they behaved as if they were walking on eggshells, afraid they would do or say the wrong thing. Elliott didn't think that was the way love should be, but since he'd never experienced it personally, he simply didn't know.

"Look, Elliott, here's the barbershop. Is yours like this one?"

The shop had only one customer, who was in the chair and covered by a cape while the barber snipped at the man's sideburns. He wondered if this barbershop did any better than his brother's in Katona Falls and if this one earned enough income to support a man with a family, even if it could never earn anything close to what a man's father-in-law might make.

He nearly stumbled at his own thoughts, but he kept walking as he spoke. "I guess they're pretty similar," he mumbled, quickening his pace.

"Elliott? Where are you going?"

He stopped abruptly to discover that they had arrived at their destination, which was next door to the barbershop.

"Is something wrong? You're being so quiet."

"No, nothing's wrong. I was just thinking."

"About what? Or should I not ask?"

He gazed into Louise's beautiful green eyes as she spoke, wondering what it would be like to come home to Louise after a hard day at work, sitting on the couch while she made dinner and little children played at his feet.

Abruptly, he looked away, back to the barbershop, whose only customer had just left. "I was thinking about things that will never happen. Now let's get that shopping done. Your mama will be unhappy if we're late for dinner." He covered his stomach with his hands and sighed, remembering the delicious roast pork Louise's mother had made last night. She'd made sandwiches with the last of the meat for their lunch today and used the most fragrant, mouthwatering bread he'd ever tasted, which he knew Louise had made. "I don't know how your family manages to stay so thin. I've never eaten so well in my life. I fear my new clothes won't fit me by the time I leave."

Louise shook her head so fast her hair flopped on her shoulder. "I doubt that will happen. But you are right. I don't want Mama to be angry, and I think she might need some items on this list for today's dinner. We had better hurry."

Elliott forced himself to put his thoughts of the future and what could never be out of his head. For the rest of the day, he would be alone with Louise, and he intended to enjoy it. Although Mrs. Demchuck said she was too busy to go with them today, Elliott highly suspected she merely wanted to spend some rare private time with her husband.

"Elliott? Are you coming?"

He turned back to Louise. Her lovely smile did strange things to his stomach, and this time, he definitely wasn't hungry.

He smiled back, determined to forget his troubles for the day. "Yes, I'm coming. Now let's have some fun shopping."

fourteen

Elliott handed John the crutches at the top of the stairs and watched John hobble into the bedroom. Elliott closed the door behind him, then made his way down the stairs and joined Mrs. Demchuck and Louise on the couch.

Besides the pleasant music of Glenn Miller, the clicking of their knitting needles added to the homey atmosphere.

"John was so tired," Mrs. Demchuck said as she turned her knitting and started another row. "But it's his own fault for insisting on walking to church. I told him that he should have let you drive him."

Elliott nodded and leaned back, letting his feet stick out straight in front of him as he linked his fingers behind his head. "I know. I told him he was going to be sorry."

Louise smiled, not missing a stitch as she spoke. "You know Papa. Once he makes up his mind, it's nearly impossible to get him to change it."

"I meant to ask you at dinner but didn't get the chance. How did your men's choir practice go?"

"Mama!" Louise laid her knitting in her lap. "It's hardly a choir. There were exactly five men. And it's called a barbershop quartet."

"But there were five. A quartet is four."

Louise resumed her knitting. "They still call it a barbershop, regardless of the number of men. It's the style rather than the number of people that determines the name."

Elliott smiled as Louise and her mother continued to banter back and forth. As the conversation progressed, he found he didn't have to say a word. Louise was doing a fine job without him, telling her mother everything that had happened, from figuring out the participants' vocal ranges, to selecting the music, to trying to show Stan Pollock when to go up and when to go down with the music in front of him.

All in all, it had been a long time since he'd enjoyed himself so much. Nick Sabinski had been correct in that he was the only one able to read music. However, that hadn't stopped the men from putting together a simple but melodious version of "Amazing Grace" in four-part harmony. Because Elliott was the only one experienced with group dynamics, they had looked to him for leadership, but it had been Louise who had held the group together with her skills on the organ, as well as her patience when they started doing more joking than singing.

As the two women continued to argue playfully over the clicking of the knitting needles, Elliott closed his eyes to think about everything that had happened that day.

At church this morning, he'd met more people, all of whom welcomed him like he belonged there. Everyone had accepted him as a friend of the Demchucks. He'd received a tentative invitation to dinner to the McSorbins' home, the family Louise had purchased her baby chickens from. Because the McSorbins had four children, the oldest of whom was Louise's friend Dorothy, he had been hesitant to accept. However, they had assured him he was welcome and they wanted to get to know him better, even though his presence in their community was temporary. The only thing he'd found odd—and realized too late to change his acceptance—was that he'd been invited without Louise.

"Hush, girl. I think he's sleeping."

He opened his eyes and smiled at Mrs. Demchuck, not moving from his stretched-out position. "No, I'm not sleeping, but I am relaxing. I was just thinking that all these years I've lived alone, I didn't know what I was missing."

Both of their mouths dropped open, and for the first time that evening, the room was silent. They'd even stopped knitting.

Elliott couldn't hold back his laughter. He sat straight and ran his fingers through his hair. "I was just teasing you. Honestly, spending a quiet evening like this is quite pleasant. I've lived alone for five years, and it's difficult to describe what it feels like to hear the sound of movement and voices around me when I'm used to only silence inside and the noise of the city outside. That changed when my brother and his family moved in with me two months ago. It's kind of relaxing, in a noisy sort of way." At the same time as he thought about his words, he also thought that listening to the sound of Louise's voice was far more pleasant than listening to the sounds of his brother back when his own family was still together under one roof.

The clicking resumed, and this time Elliott joined them in conversation as they discussed what they'd heard at church as the latest happenings in their community.

Before they knew it, it was time to go to sleep. Over the last few weeks, Elliott had learned the hard way that the seven o'clock phone call often came far too early.

❧

Louise burst in through the door, not caring that it slammed on the wall as she ran inside. At the sudden noise, the chicks in their crate beside the cookstove cheeped louder than usual. "Mama! Elliott is going to be so pleased! A letter came for him from his brother!"

Her mama smiled and wiped her hands on her apron. "Yes. He's so far from home. Do you know it's been three weeks since he's arrived? It's always good to hear from home. I remember when your father and I moved here to Pineridge, so far from our families. It was always so special to get a letter from home, but at least we had each other. Elliott has no one."

Louise was about to say that he had her but stopped. They had come to know each other quite well in the last three weeks. As well as being together every evening until bedtime, they were together almost every waking minute of every day on the weekends. Still, as much as they tried to make him feel at home with them, Louise could tell he felt awkward at times and sometimes even sad. Nothing could replace news from his family.

"Do you think he's happy here, Mama?"

Her mama rested her spoon on the cookstove. "I think so, most of the time. I suppose you've noticed that at times he seems to disappear into a world of his own."

"Yes."

"You must admit, his life has been difficult. I only hope and pray that when he leaves things will go better for him. I wonder if his brother managed to contact that friend on the coast and if there's also a letter about his other job."

Louise looked at the letter in her hand, suddenly feeling ashamed of herself. She had already been tempted to feel the thickness of the envelope to try to guess if the envelope held one letter or two, but it hadn't been a letter from his future employer she'd been thinking about. She had been wondering if there was a second letter in the envelope from a woman—a woman who would have been missing him, and conversely, a woman whom Elliott would be missing.

She laid the letter on the table as fast as if it might burn her skin. Until Elliott chose to divulge such information, such thoughts were not her business, no matter how much they disturbed her and no matter how she was coming to feel about him.

A knock on the back door made Louise glance up at the time. The freight train had arrived before the return of the section gang, and with a freight train came more hungry men.

"You're busy, Mama. I can take care of him."

As usual, Louise answered the door, spoke to the man very briefly, gave him a plate of food to eat outside, and did her best to tell the poor, bedraggled, and skinny man that Jesus loved him. He didn't look like he believed her, but hopefully one day he would remember this act of God's love for him and see that God really did care. For now, his immediate need for food had been met. When the man was done, he returned the plate, thanked her quietly, and disappeared back to the freight train. She continued to stand in the doorway as the man, plus a few others, hopped back on as the train started moving.

Louise turned and walked back into the house, closing the door behind her. "Papa and Elliott should be here soon. What can I do?"

Her mama smiled. "Set the table. As you can tell, we're having a treat for dinner today."

Louise took her time to set the table, then stood to chat with her mama about the things Mildred had told her at the post office until her papa and Elliott arrived.

She waited until she heard the thumping of Elliott helping her father up the steps stop before she opened the door. It was important for her to respect her father and not witness his difficulty, allowing him to salvage some pride after needing to be helped with the simplest things.

As soon as the door opened, her papa smiled. "Does that smell mean what I think it means?"

Elliott's brows knotted and his nose wrinkled. "Has a skunk made its home under your porch, too, now? I didn't smell it outside."

Louise laughed at Elliott's joke, then began putting the food on the table as Elliott slipped off the boots, removed his overalls, and both men washed their hands.

After they paused for a word of thanks for their meal, her mama set the rest of the food on the table.

Her papa took his portion and passed the plate to Elliott. Elliott held it for a few seconds, spooned a very small portion on to his own plate, and passed it on, as well.

Suddenly it occurred to Louise that Elliott might not have been joking about the skunk-like smell. "It's *studenetz*," she said slowly as she spooned a generous portion for herself, hoping Elliott would take her hint. "This is Mama's specialty."

Elliott looked at it, smiled hesitantly, then poked at the *studenetz* a few times with his fork before lifting a very small forkful to his mouth. With his first bite, his shoulders hunched slightly forward, his cheeks bulged slightly for a split second, and at the same time as he swallowed, he reached quickly for his coffee. Louise was about to warn him that it was still too hot to drink, but he moved too fast and drank it anyway, then flinched when he scalded his tongue.

Elliott's cheeks darkened, and he gave a forced smile to her mama, whose eyes were wider than Louise had ever seen.

"I'm very sorry, Mrs. Demchuck, but what is that?"

"It's *studenetz*. My mother taught me to make it when I was a child. It's a Ukrainian dish."

He looked down at his plate, staring at it, and saying nothing.

Louise leaned forward across the table, lowering her voice. "The English translation is pickled pig's feet."

Not only did all the high color fade from Elliott's face, his cheeks paled to a ghastly gray.

"From the pig we slaughtered last fall. We're using up last year's meat from the outdoor cellar, because soon all the snow will be melted. The weather has been too warm for it to stay frozen in there much longer."

"Pig's feet?" He gulped.

Louise lowered her voice even more. "It's not as awful as it sounds. It's just meat. The pig's feet are cleaned and singed, and they are boiled with a beef shank, onions, and spices for half a day. Then the meat is picked off the bones and put with the liquid to cool, and it turns to jelly."

The continued pallor in his face told her that he thought it was indeed as awful as it sounded.

Her mama rose from the table. "I'm sorry, Elliott. This is a very popular dish in our community, as most of the people here are of Polish or Ukrainian heritage, with some Germans.

It didn't occur to me that you wouldn't have seen it before. I'll find you something else to eat."

He stood also, lifted one hand, and made what Louise thought was a very strained smile. "No, please, Mrs. Demchuck. It's fine. You do so much for me. Please sit down and enjoy it. It's just something I've never seen before. It's good. Really."

Her mama smiled hesitantly, then returned to her chair. Everyone continued to eat their dinner, although Louise noticed that Elliott ate very little.

When the meal was done and everyone had left the table, Louise opened all the windows on the main level of the house, as well as the front and back doors to freshen up the house, despite the cool evening air.

She had almost finished drying the dishes when Elliott stepped into the kitchen. "Louise, it's okay. I didn't mean to be rude, and you certainly don't have to risk everyone catching a chill just because of me. And look at your baby chicks; they're getting cold."

Without waiting for her response, he closed the door and the windows, and immediately the house felt warmer.

"Do you make that concoction, too?"

"Yes, of course."

He opened his mouth as if he were going to say something, then closed it again and shook his head. "I'll see you soon in the living room."

With that, Elliott turned and walked away.

The rest of the evening passed quickly. No mention was made of their dinner, although Louise had a feeling her mama would not be making *studenetz* for a long time.

Since both her papa and Elliott looked tired, they all went to bed earlier than usual, but sleep eluded Louise until the wee hours of the morning. When she finally did drift off, she didn't sleep well, and it only took the sound of a small noise in the kitchen to wake her. Worried that something had happened to her chicks, Louise grabbed her robe out of the armoire and ran downstairs.

Her feet skidded to a stop in the doorway. Elliott, wearing the striped flannel pajamas he'd purchased on their first shopping trip, with his back to her, was fumbling in the dark with something at the kitchen table.

Immediately, she averted her eyes, putting all her concentration on the washstand. "Elliott! What are you doing!" she said in a loud whisper, not wanting her voice to carry upstairs to her parents' bedroom.

At the sound of her voice, the chicks cheeped louder, and whatever was in Elliott's hands clattered to the table. He spun to face her, and she couldn't help but look at him. The faint glow of the streetlamp in front of the train station coming in through the kitchen window was the only light in the room, but it was enough to show his surprise at seeing her. He glanced quickly down at his pajamas, then shuffled backward until he was against the table.

"Louise! I'm sorry. I didn't mean to wake you," he whispered back.

She clutched her robe closed around her throat and craned her neck in a futile attempt to see around him. "Are you looking for something to eat?"

"I, uh, I was hungry."

Louise couldn't contain her smile and covered her mouth with the hand not still clutching her robe closed. She forced herself not to look at his pajamas, so she stared very intently straight into his eyes and nowhere else. "I noticed you didn't eat much at dinner. If you would like, I can find some of the leftover *studenetz* for you."

"Very funny."

She giggled again. "I'm sorry. I've grown up on it. I never thought anyone would find it strange. I don't think Mama did, either. Papa just loves it."

"Does Heinrich love it, too?"

Her smile dropped. "Heinrich? Why would you think. . . ?" She let her voice trail off.

He dragged one palm down his face. "Don't mind me; I don't know if I'm more tired or hungry. Those chickens of yours woke me up, and once I was awake, my stomach wouldn't let me sleep."

"The chickens?" She glanced toward the orange crate, where she could see a few of the chicks hopping after being awakened by all the noise. It was true that they did tend to cheep a lot, but with her bedroom upstairs, the chicks in the kitchen had never disturbed her. She had not considered that their cheeping would carry into the living room and disturb him.

Guilt assailed her. "I'm so sorry about the chicks. Can I help you find something to eat? Mama has some wonderful wild strawberry jam, and there is bread from lunchtime in the bread box."

He smiled, then backed away as Louise walked to the bread box. "Thank you. But don't worry; I can do it. I ate just fine by myself when I was living alone. Please, go back to bed. I'm sorry I disturbed you."

She almost made a comment that judging by how skinny he was when he first arrived she doubted he fed himself very well but caught herself in time. It had not been lack of ability; it was lack of food.

The concept of Elliott having to go hungry almost made her ill.

She turned her head, but he remained backed up against the table.

While she would gladly have sliced the bread to make him a midnight snack, she suspected that more than really wanting to do it himself, she had embarrassed him by catching him in his pajamas.

She smiled, and he smiled back hesitantly. "Good night, Elliott. Sleep well and enjoy your snack."

fifteen

Elliott drove the spade into the ground and turned another shovelful of dirt. As he continued to dig, he ignored the tell-tale shaking of the ground. Today was Saturday. The morning track inspection was done, so he had the rest of the day off, and for today, he could ignore the trains.

He stood and wiped the sweat from his brow with his sleeve. "Is this deep enough?"

Louise leaned forward and looked down into the hole. "Yes, it is. Now come, help me split the root."

Elliott had never done any form of gardening before, but he found he didn't mind the work. It was also a good way to spend the afternoon with Louise.

Together, they tried as delicately as they could to split the large peony into two plants. Elliott was up to his elbows in dirt when a male voice sounded behind him.

"Good day, Elliott. Louise."

Both he and Louise froze and looked upward at the same time.

"Heinrich?" Elliott's head swam. "What day is it? Isn't it Saturday?"

Heinrich smiled and nodded, and Elliott immediately felt some relief, but his heart still pounded. He stood and tried in vain to wipe some of the mud off his clothes and his hands. Rather than extend his muddy hand in greeting, he crossed his arms over his chest. "To what do we owe the pleasure of this visit?"

Heinrich smiled at Louise, then turned back to Elliott, and his smile dropped. "I'd like to say that I dropped by for a simple visit, but, unfortunately, I'm here because I need to talk to you unofficially. Do you have a minute? I also need to talk to John. Do you know where he is?"

Elliott's stomach churned, and Louise's face paled.

Elliott cleared his throat. "He's in the house. I'll go get him."

He hadn't taken more than a step when Heinrich stopped him. "Wait. I think it's best we sit down and talk inside." Heinrich turned to Louise. "If you will excuse us."

As soon as they were out of Louise's range of hearing, Elliott spoke. "Is there something wrong? If there is, I take full responsibility."

"Not exactly," Heinrich replied as they walked together up the steps and into the house. "John. Good to see you."

"Heinrich?" John struggled to his feet, taking a few seconds to stop wavering on the crutches in his hurry to stand. "How did you get here?"

"Since this is an unofficial visit, I used my pass and came by the train."

"Anna! Can you make us some coffee?" John called over his shoulder, but Elliott saw that Mrs. Demchuck had already entered the room.

"Heinrich? What are you doing here on a Saturday?"

Elliott would have smiled if he hadn't been so nervous.

"There is a matter I must discuss with John and Elliott. If you'll excuse us?"

Mrs. Demchuck slipped out of the room in the blink of an eye, and Elliott's stomach flipped over a few times as John and Heinrich sat on the couch. Rather than sit three in a row, Elliott brought himself the chair from the desk.

Heinrich folded his hands in his lap. "I'll get right to the point. First of all, there was nothing wrong with the inspection or the track, so don't worry about that. However, I had to make a note of your broken leg and your new lead hand in my report, and that has drawn the attention of a few heads at the district office."

John raised one finger in the air. "Now wait a minute. I'm

authorized to do all my own hiring and firing of my section gang without anyone's permission or collaboration."

Elliott stiffened in the chair rather than let it appear like he was shrinking. Of all the things he'd tossed and turned about at night, being the cause of trouble for John at the district office was one thing he hadn't considered.

"Above everything, my only concern is the maintenance of the track, and your section is exemplary, as always. What I'm about to tell you is confidential, and I won't reveal my sources. However, if you figure it out yourself, well, that's your own reasoning. Let me say that a certain individual who heard that you fired Robert wanted the job as your lead hand. I know you are aware that your current section men get first consideration and that who gets the job is your decision."

"Yes, but nether Frank nor Henry want the job. They don't want the responsibility."

"Yes, and this person apparently knows that. He was going to apply for the job when he heard you had hired someone. Someone who has never worked for the railroad before. Someone with no experience."

"That was my choice, and I have every right to make that choice."

"Yes, you do. But be warned that this person has connections. Quite honestly, he's a good man and a good worker, and he would be an asset to your crew. What I'm trying to say is that this man, as well as others in top positions, can cause you a good deal of trouble. I'm not saying you have to let Elliott go. Considering that Elliott has no experience, I'm surprised everything has gone so well, as I know you haven't been out there working alongside him every day. I want you to consider this a friendly warning that you are going to have trouble behind the scenes, to watch for it, and to prepare yourself. I would hate for you to lose your job over this."

Elliott forced himself to breathe. His brother's letter had been brief, but in it Ike assured Elliott he had immediately forwarded his letter to Edward in British Columbia. But Elliott still hadn't heard from Edward about the logging job. If Elliott didn't hear from him, or if he received a reply that the job was no longer available, Elliott had considered staying on as John's lead hand. When the cast came off and John could manage on his own, he could simply move into the bunkhouse with Frank and Henry and hold down the job, doing as Robert, the previous lead hand, had done. At the end of the eight weeks, he would be free and would no longer have to do everything around the house and property for John, or help John over the tracks or up and down the stairs, or anything else with which he experienced difficulty.

Now, due to extenuating circumstances, this was no longer an option. He was grateful beyond words for the job John had given him, but he couldn't keep it, knowing he was the cause of dissention between John and the supervisors at the district office, who ultimately controlled John's job.

Elliott stood and cleared his throat. "Thank you for the warning, but it's not necessary. As a friend, John and I had made arrangements for me to stay only as long as he is restricted by the cast. When the cast is removed and he's back on his feet, I will be moving on, so the lead hand position will be open."

He heard John's sharp intake of breath.

Heinrich raised his eyebrows. "Really? But this is a good job and an outstanding section. John's section has won many awards in past years." He stood to meet Elliott eye-to-eye. "I know I came with a warning, but I'll be sorry to see you go. Is there another section you wanted to be working with?"

"No. It's a position not with the railroad."

Their gazes met, Heinrich nodded, and they both sat again.

"I'm glad I came. I shall make it clear at the district office meeting on Monday what your intentions are, in order for the parties involved to wind down their plans to make this an issue. How much longer does that mean that you'll be here?"

Elliott didn't need to calculate it. Even though he'd only recently considered the possibility of staying, he had been counting almost to the day his remaining time with the Demchucks. "I have four more weeks."

John didn't rise but extended his hand to Heinrich, who reciprocated it in an unspoken gentlemen's agreement.

"I really appreciate you coming out all this way on your own time to pass on that warning, and I'm glad we were able to defuse this matter before any damage was done. There must be something I can do to thank you."

Heinrich smiled and glanced outside to where Louise was busy planting her peonies. "I must admit, there is another reason I came today. With your permission, I would like to take your lovely daughter to the movie theater tonight."

❧

Louise cast her line into the water. "So the city boy does know how to fish."

He didn't look at her as he spoke. Instead, he bent his head and looked beneath him, past the trestle to the water far below, and swung his feet back and forth a few times. "I do know how to fish, but I must say, I have never had to watch the time so closely while doing it before. Fishing is supposed to be relaxing." He turned his head to stare down the length of track, then pulled her papa's pocket watch out of his pants pocket. "I'm glad this bridge isn't in your father's section," he muttered as he checked the time.

Louise couldn't hold back her giggle. While she enjoyed fishing, she'd never fished for relaxation. She fished to catch a fish. The railway bridge was the best fishing spot, as long as she was careful to be off the bridge before a train came by. Because she knew the train schedule every day, she knew in plenty of time when to get off the bridge. "If you catch something, will you be able to eat it, even after looking it in the eye?"

He grinned, and that funny thing happened in her chest

again. "You're never going to let me forget that, are you?"

She smiled back. She would never forget the day they'd gone to pick up the chicks, but soon it wouldn't matter. In under a month he'd be gone.

Something in her stomach went to battle with the lunch she'd recently eaten, and she lost her smile. She wasn't going to fool anyone, least of all herself. It did matter.

Louise turned her head and concentrated on her line in the water, far below. "Heinrich told me you aren't going to take the lead hand job on a permanent basis and that you will be leaving when Papa's cast is removed."

"That was the arrangement from the beginning."

"I was kind of hoping you'd consider staying on. Papa says you're doing a good job."

"I gave my word to Edward about the other job already. I have to admit that I briefly considered staying here, but really I can't. Besides, I won't be the cause of problems for your father because he's bent the rules for me. He's already done so much. When the time comes for me to move on, I will go—and trust that's the path God has laid out for me."

"Your decision has been made, then?"

"Yes."

There was nothing more she could say, so she remained silent.

"So how did your evening with Heinrich go?"

"Fine." It was horrible. She'd always liked Heinrich as someone her father had to answer to, but as to anything else, she had no interest. As funny as Heinrich was in a group, in private all he did was talk about himself. He was amusing to listen to, but only in the same sense as listening to an entertainer on a radio show. The conversation, what there had been of a conversation, had been all one-sided. However, if Louise wanted to be fair, she had to admit she hadn't made much effort to contribute. Heinrich was nearly fifteen years her senior. She felt the differences in the things he and his friends liked to do in their spare time. The contrast was so clear, she couldn't seriously consider him as a suitor.

Louise preferred to date men who were, and she mentally counted on her fingers, five or six years older than herself.

At first, she'd been so angry with her papa for sending her out with Heinrich that she could barely think straight. It had been so bad that she'd been forced to hold her tongue rather than be rude to Heinrich. And then, when Heinrich told her that it was definite Elliott would be leaving in under a month, she hadn't been able to think at all.

She'd been praying that Elliott could stay. She wanted him to stay on and move into the bunkhouse when her papa was out of the cast. When Elliott no longer lived under their roof, then they could start a real relationship. Until then, Elliott carefully behaved as a perfect gentleman, maintaining a careful distance, even the night she caught him in his pajamas in the kitchen. For now, it was best this way. Still, it didn't mean she had to like it.

She didn't want to be courted by her papa's supervisors. She wanted to be courted by his present lead hand.

She turned her head to study Elliott as he reeled in his line and put a new worm on the hook.

"Aren't you going to ask for more details?" she asked.

He didn't turn his head as he cast the line. "What you did is none of my business."

Louise gritted her teeth. She wanted it to be his business, but all the wishing in the world wouldn't make it so. First she'd heard it from Heinrich, now she'd heard it from Elliott himself.

He really was leaving, and there was nothing she could do about it.

"Louise! I think I caught something. Quick, get the net!"

Louise shook her head. There was something she could do. She couldn't force him to stay, but she could make the best of the time that he was here.

She grabbed the net and helped to contain the fish.

"It's just a perch. You may have caught the first one, but I'm going to catch the biggest."

He grinned at her, then froze. For a split second, she thought that if they hadn't been laden with fishing rods, and if she didn't have a squirming fish in her net, and if they hadn't been precariously seated on the railway bridge above the river that he might have kissed her.

"Is that a challenge?" he asked, but his voice carried the same husky undertone as the day he'd helped her bring home her chicks.

Louise gave him a shaky smile. "Yes." Although she had a feeling the challenge had extended beyond a little fish.

sixteen

"It's from Edward."

Elliott didn't bother to sit down, nor did he take the time to remove his boots and overalls. He wiped his hands on the rag he kept in his back pocket, then ripped open the envelope right where he stood in the doorway.

While he ripped the top, Louise stepped closer, smiling. "Mr. Sabinski teased me because this letter actually had our address on it."

Elliott smiled as he pulled the letter out of the envelope. "It was easier to just give Edward the complete address than explain why it wasn't necessary."

Louise opened her mouth, but Mrs. Demchuck's voice cut her off. "Louise! Give the man a moment in private to read his letter."

"Oops. Excuse me." She backed up, but only one small step, and waited.

Elliott skimmed the paragraphs until he found the words he wanted to read. "This is good," he said, unable to stop grinning. "The job I had originally wanted is gone, but there will be another one opening up at the time I will actually be arriving, and Edward has reserved and promised it to me. This is great! The Lord really does provide."

"That's wonderful!" said Mrs. Demchuck.

"I think I'll read the rest of the letter in the living room." He handed the letter back to Louise to hold while he slipped off his boots and overalls, and John hobbled out of the kitchen and into the living room until dinner was ready.

In his prayers before the meal, John extended an extra word of thanks for Elliott's new job opportunity and the

152

letter from his friend.

While the general mood of everyone present was of joy and genuine happiness for him, he also experienced a strange undercurrent of sadness at the same time. It wasn't until they had finished eating that he realized what it was and why.

The news also served as a final confirmation that he would, in fact, be leaving.

He didn't want to go.

Knowing the job was his also solidified in his mind that if the opportunity to stay had arisen, he would have taken it and moved into the bunkhouse and lived as the previous lead hand had done. And that way, he would have been in a position to begin courting Louise.

But that couldn't happen. Heinrich had passed on the warning, which had to be genuine and very serious for him to have come on the weekend to deliver the message unofficially.

Elliott only partially listened as the Demchucks talked about an unfortunate incident with one of the Charumkos's cows.

He didn't want to think of Heinrich, but he had to. Louise apparently had enjoyed herself with him, but then again, he'd expected she would. Not only was Heinrich a good man, but he was considerably young to be holding such an important position with the railroad. That meant Heinrich had a promising future and a very good-paying job, certainly better wages than Elliott could make at the logging camp and certainly with more stability.

He guessed that Heinrich lived fairly close to Pineridge, which meant that Louise wouldn't be too far away from her parents when they got married.

Elliott's mouthful of ham suddenly turned to cardboard. Instantly, he lost his appetite.

"Elliott? I said I have good news for you."

Elliott blinked twice in rapid succession. "Pardon me? I'm sorry. I was thinking about something else."

Louise smiled at him, her green eyes sparkling, and Elliott

temporarily lost his ability to swallow.

"I said Mama's going to do the dishes by herself tonight, because it's time to put the chicks outside."

He couldn't stop his smile. It had taken over a month, but he had finally managed to get used to the trains passing at night. He would have been able to sleep through the nights if it hadn't been for the chickens in the kitchen, scratching at the paper and cheeping and peeping at varying times during the night, then rising to full volume at the crack of daylight, which was earlier than he needed to get up.

"Yes, that is good news."

"I'll show you where Papa's cutters and the bundle of wire are."

He blinked again. "Cutters? Wire?"

Louise nodded. "Yes. You'll have to repair the holes in the fence around the chicken coop or they will escape."

"But it's Wednesday night. What about *Burns and Allen?*"

John snickered. "I'll let you know what Gracie is up to this time."

Elliott sighed. He would do anything to get rid of that annoying racket the chicks made at night, even miss his favorite radio program.

The second everyone had finished eating, Louise sprang to her feet, grabbed his arm, nearly dragging him out of the kitchen. It took him several trips to the basement and storage shed in the back of the property, but he managed to collect everything needed to repair the fencing around the chicken enclosure.

He did his best to repair the holes while Louise cleaned out the inside of the old wooden chicken coop.

Their last duty was to lay out the straw collected from the cuttings along the railroad, so the chickens could make their nests and lay their eggs.

Despite the work, Elliott enjoyed her company, even amidst the hay and chicken wire.

By the time they finished, the sun had dipped low in the west, making the skyline glow with hues of pink and purple as the sun fell to the flat prairie ground. Elliott walked carefully along the darkening ground as he carried the orange crate full of chattering and bouncing chickens out to the coop. The fuzzy little round creatures he had carried into the house not that long ago had nearly doubled in size. Now, besides the yellow fuzz, some white, black, and gray striped feathers were showing through. He also thought it was getting mighty crowded in that orange crate.

He gently lowered the crate in the straw, and Louise closed the gate behind them to prevent their escape. One by one, they released the baby chickens into their new home, then stood to watch them peck and run in the straw.

Elliott couldn't help but scratch his arms. He wondered if straw contained fleas or if it was just the dry dirt and pieces of straw that caused the itch.

"You should wash your arms right away. I know the straw can be irritating."

"You can say that again."

He stood beside Louise as her brood of chickens bounced around their feet. It wasn't like having children, but he knew these chicks were the closest he could ever come to that with Louise. He turned to tell her that he looked forward to a relatively quiet night, except for the trains, but when she raised her head toward him and smiled, his words caught in his throat.

"Well, city boy, I guess you're glad they're finally outside."

"Yes," he mumbled, then raised his hand to touch her cheek. "You have something on your face." As gently as he could, Elliott tried to brush the offending dirt, but the feel of her soft skin beneath the roughness of his own fingers distracted him.

He wanted to kiss her. But he didn't have that right.

Elliott quickly lowered his hand and stepped back. "You're right. I'd better go wash up."

And with that, he nearly ran into the kitchen.

Despite the absence of the chickens from the kitchen, Elliott knew it was going to be a long night.

❧

Louise poured the iodine onto Elliott's finger where she'd pulled out a splinter, then gritted her teeth in sympathy when he blinked repeatedly.

"All better?" she asked meekly. "You don't want it to get infected."

He blinked a few more times, then swiped his sleeve over his eyes. "Wow, that made my eyes water. But, yes. Thank you."

"Did Papa not warn you that some of the window frames were rough?"

Elliott stood at the foot of the ladder and gazed skyward, up to the window on the second story of the house. "Yes, he did, but it started to slip out of the clip, and I had to catch it quickly before it fell to the ground and broke. I've never had to take storm windows out and put up screens before. The barbershop didn't have windows that opened."

Louise glanced briefly at her papa, who was busy painting the wooden frames of the storm windows that Elliott had taken off the house while her mama diligently washed the dust off the screens before he put them up. "At least Papa is able to do something. I've never seen him enjoy painting before. I hope he doesn't get too much paint on the cast."

Her mama stood and handed Elliott the cleaned screen for her bedroom window.

Louise held the ladder steady while Elliott scaled it. He fitted the screen into place, turned the clips, then came down the ladder very, very slowly.

She could tell by his unsure footing on the ladder that not only had he not changed windows before, it didn't appear that he'd spent much, if any, time up a ladder, especially one so large. Of all he'd done for them since he'd been there, Louise thought this chore to be the most daunting for him.

Overall, she couldn't help but admire his willingness to

tackle without complaint all the jobs given to him. Since he arrived, he'd chopped all the wood they needed for the cookstove, as well as carried it into the kitchen. Then, as the weather continued to warm with the coming of summer, came the weekly chore of cutting the grass.

The last time he'd tended to a lawn had been in his teen years, when he'd lived at his parents' home. Since he moved into the upstairs suite at the barbershop, which had been a space of five years, he hadn't touched a lawn mower because being in the business area of Katona Falls, there had been no lawn. Unfortunately, it showed. Her father had to teach Elliott both how to repair and how to sharpen the blades of their lawn mower. The first time he'd done it, Louise had worried that he might be cut by the twirling blades, but of course, she'd worried for nothing.

Last week, her mama had done her spring cleaning, and she'd had Elliott help move all the furniture, including the piano, so she could wash behind everything.

All through the years, Louise had never realized the tasks her father carried out concerning the house and property, jobs neither she nor her mama could do, especially in the spring. Now, when her papa was unable to do them, she didn't know what they would have done without Elliott.

Her mother appeared at her side as she steadied the ladder for Elliott at her parents' bedroom window.

"This must be very trying for him. I can tell he's never done this before, either. His life must have been very different in the city."

Louise nodded, not letting her attention wander from Elliott, perched high above them. This time the clip to hold the storm window had rusted into place, and he was banging at it with the handle of a screwdriver to loosen it. "I couldn't believe his face when we asked him to fix the roof of the outhouse."

Her mama nodded back. "I know. But it was a job that needed doing."

Louise couldn't help her smile. "I've noticed no hesitation when we ask him to drive the car. I think driving us around is the only job he finds fun."

"Yes. He will be taking your papa to have the cast removed next Saturday morning. I think Elliott will enjoy the drive, but your papa will enjoy it more."

Something in Louise's chest tightened. Of course, she was happy for her papa that his leg was healed and he wouldn't be so restricted. The past seven weeks had been difficult for him, because as well as the cast being heavy and awkward, the last couple of weeks had been highly uncomfortable for him, just as the doctor had predicted.

Soon the cast would be removed, and there would be no need for Elliott to remain to do her father's chores for him.

Every day the calendar in her head flipped another page.

Her mama moved to the side as Elliott began to descend the ladder, balancing the storm window in his arms as he struggled to keep his footing on the ladder. "Next Sunday his barbershop quintet will be singing in church. I look forward to it. They were so beautiful the other time they sang for everyone."

"It's called a barbershop quartet, Mama."

Her mama grinned. "No, it's not. There are five of them, and that makes it a quintet." With her words, her mama fetched the next screen for Elliott to put up and left it leaning against the house. Louise held the ladder more firmly as it shook with Elliott's movements as he continued to come down.

Once his feet touched the ground, he rested the storm window against the house, picked up the screen, and ran his fingers through his hair, pushing it back off his forehead. "It's getting hot up there. Isn't this weather great?"

Louise looked into his face. Since he'd been staying with them, he'd changed so much. He'd put on some weight, and although he was still thin, he looked good, even handsome. She noticed he smiled more often, and occasionally he repeated jokes he heard, although he sometimes missed the delivery on the punch line.

In many ways, she couldn't believe he was the same man she'd found desperately eating wild strawberries, only seven weeks ago, but in the ways that counted, he was exactly that same man.

Louise felt the burn of tears starting in the back of her eyes. She couldn't let him see her cry. "You look thirsty," she mumbled. "Let me get you something cool to drink."

With that, she turned and ran to the house.

She knew at that moment, she'd fallen in love with Elliott Endicott, and in eight short days, he would be gone.

seventeen

Elliott gave the other men the signal for the close of the worship song, and they all cut off the final note at the same instant, leaving an awed silence in the sanctuary. In the back row, he could see Nick's wife dabbing at her eyes and blowing her nose. As he scanned the room, he could see many women sniffling, as well as a few of the men trying to discreetly wipe their eyes.

Elliott's step faltered slightly as he started to walk off the platform to take his seat.

This was it. His last Sunday with this church family. John's cast had been removed on Saturday. John would be using the crutches for a few more days off and on, but he was doing well. Soon he would be completely on his feet unassisted again, and life would be back to normal.

The new lead hand had arrived yesterday. They'd done the track inspection together, and as Heinrich had said, the new man was experienced and a good worker, sure to be an asset to John's section gang.

They no longer needed him. Elliott's work here was done.

Rather than prolong the agony and in order to make a clean break for the new man to start the next day, Elliott had planned not to draw out a painful departure. He would be leaving on the 3:15 train today, not as he'd come, but as a paying passenger.

He inhaled deeply and stepped down from the platform, but as he did, Pastor Galbraith called his name from the pulpit, then addressed the congregation.

"In case any of you don't know, this is Elliott's final service with us. Elliott, would you like to come and share a word with the congregation?"

Elliott's stomach clenched. He'd never spoken in front of a group before. Even though this congregation consisted of some very friendly people and he'd spoken to everyone individually at some time in the last eight weeks, the fact was that in the present situation, he would be speaking to a collective audience.

He turned around, about to decline, but everyone seated smiled and nodded at him, making it impossible to refuse.

"Hi," he mumbled.

"Speak up!" someone called from somewhere in the middle of the congregation.

Elliott cleared his throat. "I don't know what to say. I suppose I can start by saying what a blessing it's been to be a part of this fine community for the short amount of time I've been here. You've welcomed me as a friend and as a Christian brother when I was a stranger."

He smiled to the congregation, ready to step down, but the smiles and nods of many people kept his feet rooted.

He fixed his sights on a piece of paper on the pulpit and continued. "When I arrived here, I had literally nothing. I lost my job, my home; and the only family I have left has enough troubles of their own without me. I thought I was following the only option I had left, but on the way I was robbed and what little I had left was taken from me.

"I'd never imagined what it would be like to have to accept charity from strangers as a means of survival, with little or no hope in sight. It's not a pleasant place to be. I can now understand the despair and depression that drives some people to the brink of taking their own lives.

"Living off the freight trains is dangerous and difficult, and I was not prepared for what lay before me when I chose that path. In the state I was in, I'm not sure I would have survived if God hadn't placed me in the path of the Demchuck family. They fed me, clothed me, encouraged me, and treated me as their equal. They even gave me a job when I had nothing to offer in return. They gave me the means and the will to carry on when I had nothing left down to the depths of my soul."

He paused for a few seconds to compose himself, and a hushed silence permeated the crowded room.

"John, Anna, and Louise, thank you. I owe you my life."

Elliott swallowed hard, knowing he was about to lose control.

He faced the congregation, so many of whom had become more special to him than words could say.

"God bless you all, as He has truly blessed me."

Without another word, he walked quietly to his seat.

Pastor Galbraith returned to the pulpit. "There is nothing I can say today to add to that. I think I'll save this sermon for next week. If the men's group would like to return to the front for another song of praise and worship, then we'll close the service."

Elliott rose once again, and the men took their place in a row. Louise played a single chord on the organ, and they sang "Rock of Ages." As they neared the close, Elliott had to struggle not to let his voice crack. Not only was "Rock of Ages" his favorite hymn, but it was also what Louise had been humming the first time he'd met her. He found it disquieting to be singing it now, as a reminder that in an hour he would be gone and he'd never see her again.

He barely held himself together, but mustering all the strength and dignity he had within him, Elliott made it to the end of the service and endured a number of teary good-byes before he excused himself to be with Louise.

That not a word was said the entire trip back to the house seemed strangely fitting. He had so much he wanted to say, there wasn't enough time if they'd had all day.

Once they arrived at the house, he tucked his last few belongings into his new suitcase and zippered it closed while Louise watched.

"I can't really believe you're going," she said, her voice far too quiet to be Louise.

"I know. For one of the few times in my life, I'm completely lost for words."

The slam of the back door told him they were not alone. John and Mrs. Demchuck walked into the living room and stood beside him.

"Thank you for everything you've done for us, Elliott. I will always believe it was God's perfect timing to deposit you here, waiting for me, the day of my accident."

"I know. I feel the same. And I don't know how to thank you for all you've done for me, either. The Lord really does provide."

Elliott reached forward to shake John's hand, but when their hands clasped, John pulled him into a quick embrace, still holding one hand and patting him on the back with the other.

Elliott squeezed his eyes shut so he wouldn't make a fool of himself and patted John's back as well.

When he pulled himself away, he turned to Mrs. Demchuck, who was standing beside him with tears streaming down her face.

"Thank you, Mrs. Demchuck. I don't know what else to say. Except that I'll miss you."

At his words, Mrs. Demchuck flung herself at Elliott, wrapped her arms around him, and sobbed. He couldn't make out a word of what she said, so he hugged her back and said nothing. Not that he could have said anything if he wanted to.

"Anna, come with me. Elliott's train will be pulling into the station in five minutes. Let's let him say good-bye to Louise."

Mrs. Demchuck backed up and rested her palm on his cheek. "Write soon and write often. And may the Lord be with you, night and day, Elliott. Now go to the station. You don't want to miss that train."

Elliott picked up his suitcase, and he and Louise began their last trip together to the train station. About halfway there, he felt Louise's hand touch his. She linked her fingers between his, then clasped his hand. Elliott closed his fingers around hers, then gave her hand a gentle squeeze.

The train arrived at the station at the same time as they did.

He lowered his suitcase to the ground, but he didn't let go of Louise's hand.

Her lower lip quivered and one tear rolled down her cheek. "I'll miss you, city boy."

Elliott thought his heart was in a vise. Every beat hurt. He couldn't breathe. His stomach felt like a rock.

If he didn't do this now, he never would.

He let go of her hand and cupped both cheeks in his palms and brushed a few tears away with his thumb. He gazed into her beautiful green eyes one more time, his eyes drifted shut, and he lowered his head until their lips were almost touching. "I love you, Louise," he ground out in a ragged whisper. And then he kissed her with all the love and longing in his heart and empty soul.

When her arms slid around his back and tightened, Elliott thought he'd died and gone to heaven. For a second their lips separated, but he could still feel the heat of her breath on his cheek, and he didn't want to let her go.

"I love you, too, Elliott," she whispered back, and then she kissed him the same way he'd just kissed her.

"All aboard!" the conductor called out.

He struggled to get his next words out. "I have to go."

Louise stepped back. Elliott picked up his suitcase, and she walked with him to the edge of the platform. He handed the conductor his ticket.

"Luggage?" the conductor asked.

"Just one and I'm carrying it with me."

The conductor returned his ticket. Elliott started to go up into the coach but stopped on the first step. Louise shuffled forward to stand on the platform beside the steps extending from the car's entrance. He turned sideways, and with his free hand, he brushed his fingers on Louise's cheek, rubbing his thumb over the line of tears. "I'll write," he muttered, then hopped aboard the train, and took his seat.

The conductor closed the door, which brought up the steps. He pulled the cord to signal the engineer that all passengers were aboard, and the train started to move.

Elliott stared out the window, watching Louise standing on the platform getting smaller and smaller.

This part of his journey had ended, and a new one had begun.

❧

"Louise! You've got another letter from Elliott!"

Louise dropped her bucket of chicken feed, picked up her skirt, and ran to the house. In a single motion, she grabbed the envelope from her mama's hands and tore it open.

"What did he say? He's been gone over a month, yet he still must be sending three letters a week. He's sent your papa another letter this time, too, but you get far more letters from him than your papa does."

Louise only half listened as she read. She broke out into a smile as she skimmed through. "He's asking about the chickens, and he's come up with names for all of them so we won't eat them." Louise lowered the letter and grinned openly at her mama. "Before he left, I could tell he had a few favorites in the chicken coop, almost like pets."

"I suppose I'm not surprised. How is his job working out?"

Louise continued to read. "No different than his last letter. He says it's hard, but it's good, honest work." Louise stopped to giggle and covered her mouth with one hand. "He says he's put on five more pounds, and he doesn't look like a city boy anymore."

"That must mean he's keeping it on. I was worried for awhile. This is good."

"Oh! He was telling me about this in his last letter. That ministry he's developing with the other men in the logging camp—he says he's working on starting a small church there. There are also a few married couples living out there, some even with children."

"Really?"

"I've told you that before, Mama. It's a large place."

"Louise! Your chickens are escaping!"

Louise tucked the letter into her apron pocket as she ran to catch her chickens. Already, she had thought of a number of things she wanted to say to Elliott, even though she'd last mailed a letter to him only three days ago.

It nearly tore her heart out every time she mailed a letter to him, because it reminded her of how far away he was. On the other hand, reading a letter from him was almost as good as seeing him in person. They'd been pouring their hearts out to each other in their letters, to the point that Louise knew she had found her soul mate. If only he didn't live so far away.

Just as Louise caught the last chicken and returned it to the coop, the road master's car rode onto the siding, and Heinrich and her papa got out.

Louise's heart sank. She had reluctantly gone out with Heinrich once since Elliott had left, but nothing had changed, and nothing ever would. She felt nothing for Heinrich, regardless of what he felt for her.

Her papa walked inside, and Louise knew he would be getting something out of his desk before the two men went into the toolhouse to check the speedster.

Instead of waiting at the toolhouse, to her dismay, Heinrich approached her.

"Good day, Louise."

She nodded and wiped her hands on her apron. "Greetings, Heinrich."

"I don't have much time, so I'll say this quickly. As you no doubt know, I'm quite fond of you."

She could feel the heat rising in her cheeks. She didn't know what to say, so she said nothing.

"But it is more than obvious to me that your heart is elsewhere. Would I be correct to say it's far away, with Mr. Endicott, your father's temporary lead hand?"

"I'm sorry, Heinrich, that is true. I didn't mean to hurt you."

He sighed. "Such is the way of life, Louise. I know with him so far away, this has not worked out the way you would have wanted it, either, but alas, life often disappoints. I just wanted to thank you for our time together and tell you not to worry. But if one day your feelings for Mr. Endicott do change, please, let me know."

Louise smiled and reached out to touch her fingers to Heinrich's forearm. "Thank you, Heinrich," she muttered. "You are a good man, and one day, with God's blessings, that right woman will come to you."

Her papa's voice from the step stopped Heinrich before he could reply. "Heinrich! I've found that report you were looking for."

Heinrich smiled and nodded once. "Until next time, Louise."

Louise smiled, turned, and ran into the house. She didn't care that she couldn't use her papa's desk; she would sit on the floor if she had to, to write back to Elliott and get the letter away before the next train came through for the mailbag.

~

A knock on the back door nearly made Louise drop the potato she had been peeling. She glanced up at the clock, but as she suspected, according to the time, the train that had just pulled into the station was a passenger train, not a freight train. If it wasn't a hobo begging for food, she had no idea who it could be, because anyone who knew them would be knocking on the front door.

Her mama had gone upstairs to get a new apron, so Louise answered the door.

"Greetings."

"Elliott!"

Her head swam as he enveloped her in his arms, kissed

her, and twirled her around so fast her feet left the floor. The second her feet touched the floor, he kissed her again.

She wrapped her arms around the back of his neck, not wanting to let him go as they spoke. "What are you doing here? I should be angry with you for not telling me you were coming."

"I did write, but I suppose I'm on the same train as the mailbag."

He grinned, sending Louise's heart into a tailspin.

She grinned back. "We're having chicken for dinner. Are you staying?" She almost blurted out a name for the chicken she had in the oven when suddenly all foolish thoughts left her and her stomach tied into a painful knot. "Why are you here? Did you lose your job?"

Elliott shook his head. "No. The opposite, in fact. I've been promoted to a supervisory position, with the help of a good recommendation from our friend and road master, Heinrich Getz."

"Heinrich gave you a recommendation?"

"Yes. And I'm here to ask you if you'd like a job. Two jobs, actually."

"A job? But Papa wanted me to go to college in the fall, which is coming up in two weeks."

His calloused palms cupped her cheeks, and Louise leaned into his warmth.

"I've already got permission from your papa, but now, I'm going to ask you. First of all, the logging camp is in need of a head cook for the cookhouse, and I was wondering if you were interested in the job."

Louise's heart stopped, then started up in double time. "Me?"

"The homes and conditions out there are a little rough, but in many ways not too much different than this, although I hear talk of improvements happening as they continue to expand. I've experienced your cooking skills firsthand, and I've also seen the work you've done organizing the church suppers and other events for your church. I think you'd be perfect. And most of all, I think you'd enjoy it."

"I don't know. . . ."

His hands slipped to her waist and he pulled her closer. "The second job is the more important one. With every letter we exchanged and every day that went by, I knew I couldn't live without you. My future is stable now, and even though it's not the job I'd dreamed of, it wouldn't matter if I could have something far more important. What I'm asking is if you'll be my wife and come back with me to the logging camp, whether or not you want the job in the cookhouse. I want you to be there with me, at my side, as my helpmate and my friend and the mother of our children. We've got a church together, and it has a real sense of fellowship and community. Louise Demchuck, will you marry me?"

"Yes!" she squealed, then rose up on her toes to meet his kiss.

While locked in his kiss, in the back of her mind Louise heard the front door slam, followed by her papa's voice. "Louise? Anna? Where are you? Someone told me they thought they saw Elliott get off the train."

The echo of two pairs of footsteps stopped in the doorway, and to Louise's dismay, Elliott backed up and released her.

"Papa, Mama. Elliott and I are getting married."

Her mama squealed, ran to her, and wrapped her arms around Louise. "I'm so happy for you, Louise!"

Her papa started to shake Elliott's hand, shrugged his shoulders, then pulled him closer to give Elliott a suitable manly hug, still shaking one hand and patting him on the back with his free hand.

When the hugging was done, Louise backed up from her mother and stood beside Elliott. Her heart fluttered and her knees turned to jelly when she felt his arm slip around her waist. "You do know that this means I'd be taking your daughter away to the logging camp in British Columbia?"

Her mama smiled and sighed at the same time. "Of course

we'll miss you both, but I have to think of what our own parents thought when we got married and moved here to Pineridge to follow John's job. You have our blessings."

Elliott pulled her closer. "I have to warn you, the logging camp has even less conveniences than Pineridge."

Louise didn't care about conveniences. All she cared about was that God had blessed her with Elliott's return. She didn't care if they lived together in the heart of the city or in an igloo at the North Pole. She only wanted to marry him, and she wanted to marry him right away.

"Can we get married this weekend when Pastor Galbraith arrives and then go back to the logging camp together?"

He smiled, and her foolish heart fluttered, something she'd experienced a lot when she was with Elliott. "I think that's a fine idea."

"I'd love to work at the cookhouse at the logging camp. As long as in the spring, I'll be able to raise some chickens."

Elliott sighed. "One thing about that logging camp, it's at least quiet at night. But if it makes you happy, you know I won't say no to a few chickens."

"Even a few dozen chickens?"

Elliott squeezed his eyes shut, then gave her a rather weak smile. "Only if I can name them."

Louise raised her hands to his cheeks and pulled his face down to hers. Just before their lips touched, she stopped and whispered, "I love you, city boy."

A Letter To Our Readers

Dear Reader:

In order that we might better contribute to your reading enjoyment, we would appreciate your taking a few minutes to respond to the following questions. We welcome your comments and read each form and letter we receive. When completed, please return to the following:

Rebecca Germany, Fiction Editor
Heartsong Presents
PO Box 719
Uhrichsville, Ohio 44683

1. Did you enjoy reading *The Train Stops Here* by Gail Sattler?
    - ❏ Very much! I would like to see more books by this author!
    - ❏ Moderately. I would have enjoyed it more if

    _____

    _____

2. Are you a member of **Heartsong Presents**? Yes ❏ No ❏
    If no, where did you purchase this book?_____

    _____

3. How would you rate, on a scale from 1 (poor) to 5 (superior), the cover design?_____

4. On a scale from 1 (poor) to 10 (superior), please rate the following elements.

    _____ Heroine   _____ Plot

    _____ Hero   _____ Inspirational theme

    _____ Setting   _____ Secondary characters

5. These characters were special because_____

_____

_____

6. How has this book inspired your life?_____

_____

_____

7. What settings would you like to see covered in future
   Heartsong Presents books?_____

_____

_____

8. What are some inspirational themes you would like to see
   treated in future books?_____

_____

_____

9. Would you be interested in reading other **Heartsong
   Presents** titles?   Yes ❑   No ❑

10. Please check your age range:
    ❑ Under 18   ❑ 18-24   ❑ 25-34
    ❑ 35-45   ❑ 46-55   ❑ Over 55

Name _____

Occupation _____

Address _____

City _____ State _____ Zip _____

Email _____

Romance
on the Rails

*T*rain travel promises speed, convenience, and adventure for Americans of the nineteenth century. But four young women are carrying excess baggage on their journeys. Uprooted from secure homes and forced to reexamine their positions in life, can any of them entertain *Romance on the Rails?*

Will the swaying of the coach and the clickety-clack of the train wheels lull these young women into a dream world of false romance? Or will God show them a love as strong as the steel rails on which they ride?

paperback, 352 pages, 5 ¾₁₆" x 8"

·······Presents·······